This man looked capable of hoisting the world and playing ball with it

Beard stubble shadowed his jaw. Dark hair spilled over a glowering brow. Eyes, the color and warmth of ice, speared Dana, pinning her to the metal chair. He emanated the menacing power of a caged tiger.

"Did you waive your right to have an attorney present during questioning?"

"No," Dana said coolly.

The man tossed a briefcase onto the table. "Rule number one. From now on you don't say anything unless I'm in the room with you. Got it?"

"Who are you?" Dana said. "I want my attorney."

"Kurt Saxon." He thrust out a hand that was twice the size of hers, burned to mahogany by sun and rough with calluses. "*I'm* your attorney."

L.C.

Dear Reader,

I love my readers, but boy, some of you can ask hard questions. Recently, a young woman wrote and asked, "Don't you go stir-crazy with so much solitude? How do you stand being alone all the time writing your books?" That started me thinking about how very much *una*lone I am. I have the thousands of books, and their wonderful authors, which amuse, inspire and teach me every time I turn a page. I have my good friends, Betty, Barbara and Jule—hard-working writers—ready to offer encouragement, hand-holding, advice and bald truths when I need them. I can't forget my family, either, who are terrific about reminding me what a love story really is. (A word of caution to anyone contemplating self-employment: home offices have almost magical magnetic powers.) Then there are the folks at Harlequin: my editors, the art department, the marketing people and everyone else who helps take my words and transforms them into a lovely, solid book. Last, but most important of all, there is you, the reader. As long as I have you, I'm never without someone to talk to. And I love every minute of it. So if you want to say hello, or ask a tough question, write to me at P.O. Box 310, Monument, CO 80132-0310. I'll answer as best I can.

I sincerely hope you'll enjoy *Dark Knight,* the first of two books in the subseries I've titled MIRROR IMAGES. Next month, in August, *Dark Star* will appear in the Intrigue series.

Love and best wishes,

Sheryl Lynn

Dark Knight
Sheryl Lynn

Harlequin Books

TORONTO • NEW YORK • LONDON
AMSTERDAM • PARIS • SYDNEY • HAMBURG
STOCKHOLM • ATHENS • TOKYO • MILAN
MADRID • WARSAW • BUDAPEST • AUCKLAND

This book is for Tristan and Abby for being themselves;
and Tom for going above and beyond;
and with special thanks to Julianne,
for knowing when to say,"That stinks. Try again."

ISBN 0-373-22331-5

DARK KNIGHT

Copyright © 1995 by Jaye W. Manus

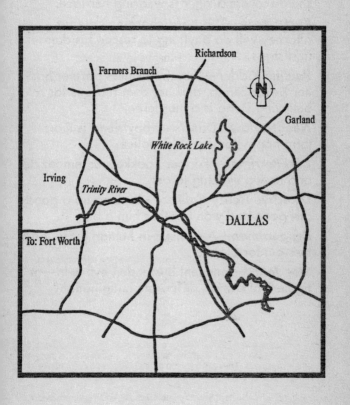

CAST OF CHARACTERS

Dana Benson—She lives the perfect life, until she discovers a killer is wearing her face.

Kurt Saxon—This hard-charging defense attorney will do anything to rescue his damsel in distress.

Pauline Kidder—Dana's business partner has her own agenda, and her own reasons for believing Dana is a murderer.

Neal Harlow—Dana's ex-boyfriend is more than happy to help...the police.

Carl Perriman—Former bookkeeper, embezzler and now a walking target.

Detective Henry Callister—Locking up a good girl gone bad won't bother him a bit.

Dragon-man—A monster in human guise, and he's out for blood.

Star Jones—Innocent bystander, evil twin—or figment of Dana's desperate imagination?

Chapter One

"Dana! I sent the only copies to Dana Benson at Star Systems. I swear, the only ones." The young man wrapped both arms around his head and curled his legs into a fetal position. "Don't hit me again," he whispered. "Please don't hit me anymore. I gave you everything. Everything!"

"Think this squirrel is telling the truth, Drag?" Eddie flexed his fingers as he studied the carnage he and his partner had wreaked in the apartment.

Dragon-man kicked an overturned lamp, shattering the ceramic base. Shards pattered the wall like shrapnel. He ground a camera lens under his boot heel. The glass squeaked.

The man on the floor whimpered. "I'll give you whatever you want. Money, anything. You can have it all. Please, just don't hurt me anymore."

Dragon-man grunted. "Hey, buddy," he drawled. "We just want what's ours." He fanned an array of photographs. The packet from the supermarket where the film had been developed had been checked off for twenty-four prints, two copies each. He counted the photographs one more time: twenty-four. He counted the negatives, too, before replacing them inside the packet. He handed Eddie a roll of silver duct tape. "Do him up, man."

After his partner trussed up their victim, Dragon-man crouched. He poked the man's battered face with the barrel of his nine-millimeter Hi-Point. "Know what's wrong with America, buddy?"

Sweat made the young man's face glow as if oiled. His eyes were black and glazed behind puffed lids. His narrow chest heaved.

"Nosy punks who can't keep their cameras outta other people's business," Dragon-man answered. "Did you think I wouldn't find you? Sneaking around in the bushes, popping off pictures. What you thinking, anyway? You a superhero or something? Trying to take a bite outta crime? You ain't that slick, buddy, you ain't slick at all."

"Hey, Drag, check it out." His partner held a photo album. He pointed to a photograph of a laughing blond woman holding a large white bass. The woman wore cutoffs and a T-shirt. In the background, lake waters gleamed gray. The caption read. "Dana and dinner."

Dragon-man pushed upright and took the picture out of the album. He gestured with his gun. "You and that camera are busy little bees, ain't ya? Let's hope this cutie-pie is more cooperative than you. I hate beating up chicks. They make too much noise."

The young man rolled his eyes.

"I know what you're asking. You want to know if I'm coming back. You betcha, buddy. If your lady friend is smart enough to give up the pictures, I'll be a nice guy and kill you quick. But if she don't . . ." He clucked his tongue. "You're gonna see me get mad, and that ain't pretty. Right, Eddie?"

"Oh, yeah, not pretty at all."

DANA BENSON SORTED through the day's mail. The secretary was out running an errand, so Dana sat behind the desk, manning the phones.

The secretary walked into the office. Only Jilly's eyes were visible above her armload of boxes. Dana hurried to help her with the supplies. The two women stacked the file folders, envelopes and stationery next to the desk. Jilly wiped her face with the back of her hand.

"Turned hot out there today. Whew!" She peeled off her jacket and grimaced as she plucked her blouse away from her sides. "I hate Dallas in the springtime. If it ain't too cold, it's too hot. Wind blowing all the time. Got another thunderstorm coming up. I swear! I never know how to dress."

"You ought to move to Hawaii," Dana said, and handed over a postcard. It showed an idyllic beach scene with blinding white sand, palm trees and a sapphire ocean. "We're getting postcards every day. I think my mother is gloating just a little bit."

Jilly read the note from Greta Benson. "I say she has a good reason. Two whole weeks in Hawaii." Her dimples deepened in an impish grin. "And I bet your dad still looks good in a bathing suit." She giggled. "Hoowee, he's the original silver-haired fox."

Dana shook a finger in mock admonishment. "I'm going to tell Daddy you have a crush on him."

Jilly's smile turned tremulous. Her chin quivered. She stared at the postcard picture as if she wanted to crawl into the scene.

Dana cocked her head. For days Jilly had been in a strange mood. More than once Dana noticed her on the verge of tears. Her normal cheerfulness seemed strained. "Is there a problem? Do you need to talk about it?"

"Dana! I have to talk to you." Pauline Kidder strode into the reception area. With each bouncy step, her ID badge flapped against her breast. She clutched a memo in her left hand and gestured wildly with her right.

Jilly looked ready to bolt, making Dana wonder if perhaps her partner weren't the cause of the secretary's odd mood.

When Pauline reached the desk, Dana extended a brightly colored postcard depicting a Hawaiian flower market.

"Mom sent you a postcard."

Looking torn between wanting to yell and wanting to look gracious, Pauline snatched the postcard and flipped it over to read the message. "Must be nice, some folks having the bucks to go gallivanting around Hawaii."

Dana caught the peevish note in Pauline's voice. There would be no sweet-talking her partner out of a bad mood today. She finished sorting the mail. Most of it was bills or invoices. She left those for Jilly to take care of. She kept advertisements, catalogs and a five-by-seven-inch envelope addressed to her in care of Star Systems Data Storage. There was no sender's name, but the Garland address was vaguely familiar. The envelope had Urgent and Personal printed all over it.

"I haven't had a vacation in eight years." Pauline cast a glare at her postcard before tucking it into her jacket pocket. She used both hands to brush back her fiery red curls. "The way things are going around here, maybe I never will."

"Jilly, hold my calls. Step into my office, Pauline."

The telephone rang and Jilly scooted around the desk to answer.

"Come on," Dana said to her partner. "Let's talk."

Jilly put the caller on hold. "It's Neal Harlow."

"Take a message. Tell him I'll call him back."

The secretary averted her gaze and her cheeks darkened. "Uh...he asked for Pauline," she said sullenly.

Dana's lips tightened. An attorney, Neal handled Star Systems's legal business. For the past few months, he and Dana had been a steady couple. That is, until over a romantic candlelight dinner at Waverley's, Neal had proposed. Not marriage, but that they live together. Dana had been trying to decide if she loved the handsome young attorney. His proposition, along with his admission about being uncertain if he were ready for a major commitment—meaning she could provide sex and laundry service until he figured it out—had decided her.

He hadn't spoken to her since.

"Tell him I'll call him back," Pauline said. Without looking at Dana, she swept into the office.

Pretending not to see Jilly's apologetic face, Dana entered the office and closed the door. "What is it this time?" she asked wearily.

In the past few months Pauline's temperament had undergone a shift from hot-tempered to plain old bad-tempered. Hardly a day passed when Pauline didn't pick a fight with Dana or one of the employees. Dana sensed her friend was under some kind of stress, but Pauline refused to talk about it.

Maybe it was time to call it quits. Time to move on to something else. Her father had semiretired, and his hints concerning her taking over Benson Realty were growing broader. Selling real estate might be a nice change of pace.

And she suspected Pauline wouldn't argue too hard about Dana leaving.

The redhead paced, her petite body fairly quivering as she gestured wildly. "It's Wainwright. You cannot give them that kind of price break!" she cried. "Are you crazy?" She flung the memo onto Dana's desk.

Dana flopped onto her chair. She managed to keep a mild expression on her face, but inside her stomach churned and her diaphragm tightened. She used a letter opener to slit the envelope marked Urgent and Personal. "The price break is only an introductory offer."

"You're talking thirty percent. We can't afford it." Pauline paused beside a small, framed Moseby Harrison sketch. Dana could almost see her inner calculator totting the price. "Our overhead is way too high."

"Wainwright Shipping is the biggest trucking outfit in the state of Texas. Once we get their business, we'll keep it. It isn't as if they'll store some of their data here and some of it elsewhere. We need their account, even if it means cutting our profit initially. It's good business, if for nothing else than the number of referrals and the word of mouth we'll get. We can't be short-sighted for the sake of a few quick bucks."

Pauline whirled. "Yeah, yeah, we have to do something, even if it's wrong. No guts, no glory. Always the big picture." She looked ready to spit. "Spare me! I am not in the mood for your rosy optimism and pep talks. We can't afford it and that's that."

"We can't afford to lose Wainwright. I understand your concerns, but we're doing okay. Really."

"That's easy for you to say. If we go bankrupt, you've always got daddy to pick up the slack."

That stung. Dana focused on the envelope.

"Unlike you, I don't have rich parents who'll keep me off the street if Star Systems goes down the tubes."

"You're being unfair. I work just as hard as you do." It took a lot of effort to keep the hurt out of her voice.

Pauline raked both hands through her short hair, fluffing her springy curls. She tugged at her jacket and fussed with a button on her blouse. "You always sound so reasonable. Everything makes so much sense when you say it. Then you spend, spend, spend."

"I'm not reckless. In the past year, business has almost tripled. We're upscaling our client list." She snatched up a story about Star Systems she'd clipped from yesterday's newspaper. In the accompanying photograph, she and Pauline stood together like the best of friends. The sight of it caused a catch in her throat. Their friendship was disintegrating, and quite possibly their business partnership, too, and she couldn't figure out why. "We're getting good coverage. Now, be straight with me. What's the real problem? Why are you so angry?"

She started to retrieve the envelope contents when it occurred to her she did know the sender: Carl Perriman. Talk about lousy timing. Pauline was on the warpath and Carl was sending packages. She slipped the envelope into her desk drawer.

"Well?" she prodded gently.

Some of the fire faded from Pauline's eyes. She plopped onto a chair and let her head fall back so she stared at the ceiling. "Good gawd," she murmured. "I'm putting in seventy hours a week, I've got no social life, my town house stinks, the techs have more personal problems than a dog's got fleas, and I'm supposed to be big sister or their mama depending on who it is."

Dana used her fingertips to smooth out the crumpled Wainwright memo. "We'll hire you an assistant. Nobody expects you to be in six places at once. We'll find somebody to pick up the slack."

"Not another employee! We can't afford it."

"We can, too. Especially if it helps you out. It won't hurt you to delegate a little responsibility every once in a while."

"If you really want to do me a favor, get rid of Jilly."

Dana was shocked. Pauline had never particularly liked Jilly, who was younger, cuter and adored by all the employees. Still, she'd never indicated she had a real problem with the secretary.

"She's sneaky and dishonest. I don't trust her. Always snooping around, talking behind my back." She shook a finger at Dana. "She and Carl Perriman had a thing going. Did you know that? For all we know she was stealing us blind, just like he was. I think they were in cahoots."

Discovering her bookkeeper and good friend had embezzled company funds had been the lowest point in Dana's life. Firing Carl had been the hardest thing she'd ever done. It had broken her heart. She had no intention of ever going through anything like it again. "If you have a problem with Jilly, then we'll work it out."

"I don't like her."

"I do. She's a terrific secretary, and I don't have a single complaint about—"

A soft knock preceded the door opening and Jilly peered into the office. "Excuse me, Dana, there are two gentlemen here to see you."

"Not now," she said. "Ask them if they can wait."

"They're policemen."

Jilly's round face had lost its peaches-and-cream coloring; it looked like paste. Before Dana could question her, two men shoved their way into the office. Dana rose and smoothed her skirt with a tug.

Pauline straightened on the chair. Her eyebrows knit into a ferocious scowl.

One man was quite tall, but so stooped his suit jacket pleated against his rounded shoulders. The other man was short and heavy-set. They separated, moving to either side of the office.

The first thing Dana thought of was that something had happened to her parents. Images of heart attacks, muggings, plane crashes or boating accidents made her throat constrict. The policemen were so stone-faced, her knees wobbled and she grasped the edge of the desk for support. "May I help you?"

Not Mom and Daddy, she prayed. Dear God, don't let anything happen to them.

"Please step around to the front of the desk, miss," the tall man said. It sounded like an order and nothing at all what a conveyor of bad news might say.

Dana glanced at Pauline, but she looked even more confused than Dana felt. "Who are you? Why are you here?"

While they showed their badges, the tall man repeated his order for her to move around the desk. The look in his eyes and the tone of his voice gave her the idea he'd come after her if she didn't comply. She moved around to the front of the desk.

"I'm Detective Henry Callister." He jerked a thumb at the short man. "Detective Al Tannenbaum. You are Miss Dana Elaine Benson?" She barely had time for a nod before he continued, "Miss Benson, I have a warrant for your arrest."

Uncertain she'd heard him correctly, she shook her head. "What?"

Pauline clapped a hand over her mouth. Her eyes sparkled. "Joke, right?" she said through her fingers. "Who are you really? Those are phony badges. Let me see those things."

"Keep your hands where I can see them," the detective ordered. He suddenly thrust a hand at Pauline. "You! Don't move."

All humor fled from Pauline's expression.

Dana pulled her hands away from her jacket pockets. Nothing had happened to Mom and Daddy. Relief relaxed her throat. Knowing this gentleman had made some sort of mistake relieved her even more. "Might I ask why you're arresting me?"

"Suspicion of murder."

Chapter Two

Detective Callister pulled a card from his pocket. "You have the right to remain silent—"

Incredulous, Dana stared at the police detective. "Are you sure you have the right person? Nobody I know has died." She looked past him to the doorway. Jilly swayed and the whites showed all the way around her irises.

Callister made a patient sound. "Miss Benson, you have the right to remain silent—"

"This is absurd. You've obviously confused me with someone else."

The short detective moved in, handcuffs ready. At the rattle and sight of them, Dana shut her mouth. Oh, but no, it had to be a joke.

But the handcuffs were very real. Tannenbaum fastened them on her wrists.

Callister read rapidly from the laminated card and asked if she understood her rights as he had stated them. Staring at the handcuffs, she nodded.

"Answer me, Miss Benson."

"Yes! I understand." She didn't understand any of this. "Pauline? Do you know anything about this?"

Where Dana was tall and easygoing, Pauline was five feet three inches of pure fire. She bristled—even her hair seemed to stand on end. "I'm fixing to find out! This is the damned stupidest thing I ever heard in my life."

"Shut up, or I'll arrest you for interfering with a police officer." Callister produced a tri-folded sheet of paper. "This is a search warrant." He unfolded it and began reading aloud.

All Dana could do was listen incredulously as he explained his intention to search the offices of Star Systems Data Storage, her automobile and her home. When he told her to sign the warrant, she did so. Her hand trembled so badly her signature looked as if it were written by a child.

Glaring at the detectives, Pauline snatched a pen. "Where are you taking her?"

Tannenbaum gave her the address of the police station at Main and Stone. He then had the audacity to request Dana's keys. He made her sign a receipt for them.

"Call Neal," Dana said. She made herself calm down. This was a mistake, that was all. "Neal will get this straightened out."

Pauline gestured wildly at Callister. "Y'all aren't getting away with this. We'll sue! This is false arrest."

"One more word, miss," Callister warned evenly.

Pauline spun on her foot and nearly knocked into a uniformed police officer. She cried, "Oh! I'll sue the pants off every one of you!" She stomped out.

Dana allowed herself to be led out of the office by a pair of uniformed officers. The three of them rode the elevator down to the lobby. When the elevator doors swished open, Dana balked. People were staring. Dana had at least a passing acquaintance with most of the tenants. Unfortunately, few knew her well enough to realize this was all an unfortunate mistake.

Trying to hide the handcuffs under her jacket and lowering her face so her hair swung over her cheeks, she crossed the lobby. A light flashed and she jerked her head up. A man aimed a camera at her face and took another picture. The police officers ordered the reporter out of the way.

Only when they reached the patrol car did Callister's words truly sink in. Murder. Dana Benson, also known as Princess to her parents, was being arrested for murder.

It had to be a joke.

The punch line failed to materialize as she rode in the back of the patrol car. Nor was there anything funny at the police station. There, an officer took her fingerprints, a photographer took mug shots, another officer took down her vital statistics, and another took away her silk scarf, handbag, jewelry and watch.

She kept glancing at doorways. At any moment now, Neal Harlow would come charging to the rescue.

"You can make a phone call, Miss Benson," the booking officer said. She indicated a telephone on the desk.

Dana called the office, and when Jilly answered, she said, "Neal isn't here. Where's Pauline? Did she reach—"

"Dana!" Pauline said breathlessly into the telephone. "I talked to Neal. He said he doesn't handle criminal cases—"

"Criminal?" Dana blinked rapidly. This was a mistake, not a criminal matter. "Where is he?"

"I'm trying to explain. Neal doesn't handle criminal cases. So he's calling another attorney. He'll be there as soon as he can. Hang in there, kid." Her harsh, bitter laugh rasped through the phone lines. "Those sons of bitches are going through the classified storage area! Good gawd almighty! I'm about fixing to do some murdering myself."

Neal wasn't coming? Had she hurt him so badly he'd actually abandon her?

Pauline promised she'd move heaven and earth to make sure Dana was free within the hour. She also swore those blasted cops would be eating their words and nasty attitudes for dinner.

The police officer made her sit on a bench and shackled her left wrist to the armrest. Dana stared at the handcuffs, unable to believe Neal had refused to come to her aid. Fine, their breakup hadn't been exactly congenial, but he was still her attorney. Professionally he was bound to help her.

Police officers walked past her. A few stared openly at the length of leg exposed by her skirt. A man wearing handcuffs, being led down the hall by a policeman, leered at her. "Hey, blondie," he said, "don't know what you did, but please do it to me." Even the policeman laughed.

Face flaming, she slumped on the bench. She glared at the ink staining her fingernails but doubted the police would have the decency to allow her to wash her hands properly.

A police officer finally unlocked the handcuff from the bench. Dana glanced at a wall clock, noting she'd been sitting on the hard bench for more than an hour. It was about time they got this mess straightened out.

Instead, the officer led Dana down a hall.

Callister waited for her in a small, bare room without windows. The unshielded lights overhead gave everything a greenish glow. Dana warily eyed the other women in the room. All of them were tall like her; all were blondes. Dana tugged at her linen suit jacket. Callister removed her handcuffs and gave her a small rubber band. He told her to tie back her hair.

"Not with this," she said. "It'll break my hair."

"Tie it back. Now."

She put her hair in a loose ponytail. He handed her a white card marked with a number three.

"This is a lineup, Miss Benson." Callister pointed. "You will proceed in order through that door. Find the number three on the floor and stand on it, facing front. Hold up your numbered card and follow directions."

She opened her mouth to argue, but his hard eyes, dark and probing as a predatory bird's, stopped her. She feared she might get sick. Swallowing the unpleasant watering in her mouth, she followed numbers one and two through a door.

The lineup room was narrow with a glass wall. She had to climb two stair risers to reach a platform. Behind the platform the wall was marked with heavy black lines showing inches and feet in bold numerals. She found the number three and stood on it and held her card at chest level.

Sweat trickled into her eyes. A disembodied voice ordered all of them to face left. Shoes scuffled on the wooden platform. The voice ordered them to turn around so they faced the door. Then again it told them to face the front.

Were the other women under arrest, too? The idea of being in the company of criminals made Dana's flesh crawl.

"Number three, take two steps forward."

The voice repeated the command twice before Dana realized he meant her. She stepped forward. She tried to see past the glass, but the room behind it was darkened and the bright lights shining on her face made it impossible to see anything. She could feel watching eyes.

"Step back, number three."

After going through the right-face, left-face, step-forward and step-back routine several times, the voice dismissed them. They filed out of the room. Several of the women smiled and joked with the female police officer. One held out her hands and was handcuffed. Dana hoped she could now leave. Surely they must realize their mistake by now.

Instead, she was handcuffed again and led to another room. This one was about eight feet wide and ten feet deep, containing a sturdy metal table and several chairs. One of the industrial gray walls had a mirrored glass window she suspected allowed whomever was on the other side to observe her. The tile floor was gouged and stained, suspiciously yellow in spots. Her nose wrinkled at the sweaty stink underlying the stench of disinfectant.

Without her watch, she didn't know how long she waited. She sat for a while. She paced, but the dirty walls intimidated her. The handcuff chain rattled, getting on her nerves. The door had a tiny glass insert, but the only thing she could see was the wall on the opposite side of the hall. Chilled by the idea of someone watching her, she avoided looking in the mirrored glass.

Finally the door opened. Even Callister's grim, narrow face was a welcome sight.

His partner, Tannenbaum, placed a cassette recorder on the table. He tested it before he perched on the table beside it. Callister drew up a chair and sat on it backward. He placed a sheet of printed paper on the table along with a yellow legal pad and several pens.

She could hear her own heartbeat pulsing in her ears.

"You're in a lot of trouble, Dana." Callister's voice was flat and toneless. "Let's talk about it."

Tears scratched her eyes. But darn it, they were not going to make her cry. She lifted her chin. "I have told you, you've made a mistake. There's nothing to talk about."

Callister turned the sheet of printed paper and pointed to the first line. He urged her to pick up a pen.

"Let's go through your rights again. Do you read English, Dana?"

"Of course I read English. I have a degree in business administration."

Tannenbaum cracked a smile. He seemed a lot friendlier than his partner. At least, he didn't look at her as if she were public enemy number one.

As Callister read each right, he asked her to initial the line. When he finished, he asked her to sign the paper. "Now, you understand fully your rights as I've explained them to you. So—"

"I want an attorney." She wanted to cross her arms, but the handcuffs prevented her. She crossed her legs, instead. "I want him right now. I will not say another word until he gets here. Since you won't listen to me, then he can straighten this out."

Callister rasped a hand over his jaw. "That might take a while."

She interpreted that to mean a long while. "You have humiliated me in front of my entire office. I will not be bullied further. I want my attorney." She braced for anger.

Instead, Tannenbaum slipped off the table. He unplugged the tape recorder and coiled the cord. Callister gathered the legal pad, rights statement and pens. Astonished to have won a round, Dana almost smiled.

"We just want to hear your side of it. That's all." Tannenbaum graced her with a sheepish smile. "But, we understand. No hard feelings."

"My side of what?"

"Your side of the story, Dana."

"I don't have a side of the story. I don't know what you're talking about."

Tannenbaum blinked innocently at his partner. "You don't think we've made a mistake, Henry. Do you?"

"She's just being stubborn." He spoke over the top of her head. "Maybe she don't know how stubborn we are."

Dana stood. She was taller than Tannenbaum, so she leaned on the table to meet him at eye level. "How many times do I have to tell you, this is a mistake. I haven't killed anybody. Ever. Ask anyone."

"I want to ask you." Tannenbaum had a soft voice, his accent as warm and thick as home-baked bread. Under other circumstances she might think it was a nice voice. "But we've got lots of time. The dead guy's not going anywhere."

She flinched.

Callister flipped a hand. "Let's grab some lunch. We got a lot of other stuff to do."

"Isn't my attorney here yet?"

Tannenbaum shrugged. "I haven't seen him. What about you, Henry? Ah, you know how those guys are. Time is money in their pockets. They always take forever to get around to anything. Don't worry, he'll be here in a couple of hours. Tomorrow morning at latest."

Her knees wobbled and she had to sit down again. "I can't stay here all night."

Tannenbaum put the tape recorder on the table. "Hey, with a lawyer, without a lawyer, you're going to talk to us, right? I mean, how can we clear up this *mistake* if you don't tell us what happened?''

"But nothing happened."

"So what's the harm in telling us about it?"

He had a point there. She shifted uneasily on the chair. She wasn't guilty, so she didn't actually need an attorney. She wondered if her insistence on an attorney made them think she was guilty.

A knock on the door made both detectives turn around. Callister beckoned to his partner. Tannenbaum gathered all the pens but left the legal pad and tape recorder on the table. The men left her alone.

Enough time passed for her to start sweating. She caught herself watching the bare fluorescent bulbs and wondering what would happen if the building lost power and the lights went out. Claustrophobia sneaked its way into her chest and belly.

The door opened and large brown fingers curled around the edge. "I won't tolerate your Gestapo tactics, Callister." A man pushed the door open.

Dana cringed. Tannenbaum with his soft voice and false friendliness was bad, humorless Callister was worse, but this man went beyond the realm of awful. He was as tall as Callister, but where the policeman looked as if the weight of the world crushed his shoulders, this man looked capable of hoisting the world and playing ball with it.

She'd made them angry and now they were sending in the big guns.

He swung his head around to face her. Beard stubble shadowed his jaw and dark hair spilled over a glowering brow. Eyes, the color and warmth of ice, speared her, pinning her to the metal chair.

"Are you Dana Benson?"

She nodded and sank lower on the chair.

"Did you waive your right to have an attorney present during questioning?" He emanated the menacing power of a caged tiger.

Oh, no, she thought frantically. Please, dear God, do not leave me alone in this room with this man. "No," she squeaked. "Sir. I want my attorney."

He yelled over his shoulder. "I'll have you up on charges, Callister. Now, get the hell out of here." He walked inside and slammed the door. He tossed a briefcase onto the table. It clattered and she nearly fell off the chair.

"Did you give them a statement? Sign anything? Did they tape-record anything you said?"

She shook her head, then remembered the statement she'd signed and nodded. Except, that was only a statement of her rights, so she shook her head again.

He rumbled a noise thick with disgust. He slapped the table and made it jump. He made Dana jump. "Rule number one, from now on you don't say anything unless I'm in the room with you and tell you to speak. And you don't sign anything. Got it?"

That seemed like a very odd thing for a police officer to say. "Who are you?"

He thrust out a hand that was twice the size of hers, burned to mahogany by the sun and roughened with calluses. "Kurt Saxon. I'm your attorney."

Dana struggled to find her composure and make sense of this new development. She refused to believe this rough, uncouth... *creature* was an attorney. Attorneys wore tailored suits and polished shoes; this man's suit jacket looked slept in, not to mention his wearing it over a T-shirt, a rumpled dress shirt and a pair of jeans streaked with reddish mud. And he wore athletic shoes!

"Where's Neal Harlow? He's my attorney."

"Neal is a corporate suit. I handle criminal defense. You don't like me, fine. We'll get you out on bail, then you can find somebody you do like." He opened the briefcase. Only one latch worked. The other looked as if it had been torn off in a fit of fury.

He swept the tape recorder aside and plopped a legal pad onto the table. He scrounged through his pockets for a pen. He scribbled on the pad, but the pen didn't work. He tossed it on the table and found another pen.

Without looking at her, he said, "Full name, address, the usual."

He sounded like a drill sergeant. Her mouth fell open. She stared at the mirrored window, praying someone was watching in case she needed protection from this dangerous-looking man.

"Full name? Any aliases?"

She gave a start. "Uh, Dana Elaine Benson. And I do not have an alias. You want my address?"

Still not looking at her, he nodded. She gave him her home and business addresses. He fired more questions at her. Age. Birth date. Social security number. Place of business. Did she own or rent. What about family in the area. Arrest record. As she answered his questions, her resentment swelled. He acted worse than the police. At least they'd been polite.

Kurt glanced at his watch. "It'll be about four hours before I can get you in front of the magistrate." He huffed a dry laugh. "At least it gives us time to talk. Tell me about the shooting. Who is he to you?" He finally looked at her.

She met his inquisitive gray eyes. She hadn't understood a single word he'd said, and furthermore, she didn't want to. Neal had done this to her. He'd sent this blustering oaf to teach her a lesson.

"Talk to me, Dana. Even if you get another attorney, client-attorney privilege holds. I need to know everything."

Her stomach churned. "I need to visit the ladies' room."

He went to the door and tore it open. His harsh actions made her cringe. He possessed all the finesse of a professional wrestler.

"My client needs to hit the head," he announced loudly.

Dana jumped to her feet. "Mr. Saxon! I will not have you bellowing about my private matters."

He looked over his shoulder. "This isn't luncheon at the country club. It's a police station. You need to go, do it."

Nobody spoke to her in that tone of voice. She raked him from head to toe with a contemptuous glare.

"I am," she said coolly, "well aware this is not a country club. And I will thank you to be aware that as my attorney, for however short a period that may be, you are in my employ. You will show me a little respect." She stalked out of the interrogation room, and a waiting police officer took her arm.

Chapter Three

Kurt waited until the door closed before he let a low, admiring whistle escape. He hadn't seen a class act like that since Princess Grace of Monaco had passed away. Dana Benson reminded him physically of the actress-turned-princess, as well. Tall, slim and icy blond, she possessed a cool elegance many tried, but usually failed, to achieve. He shook himself and returned to the table. Too bad she had a first-degree murder charge hanging over her head.

When she returned, her eyes were red and swollen, but she glided into the room like a queen ascending her throne. He bounced a foot on his knee and played a tattoo with his fingers on the tabletop. Her gelid gaze skimmed over his athletic shoe. Her disapproval shone through loud and clear. What did she expect? Neal had reached him in the middle of playing catcher in a softball game, and he hadn't wasted time with a shower and a fresh change of clothes.

The policewoman moved to put the cuffs back on Dana's wrists.

Kurt waved a hand. "Beat it with those, Patty."

Patty grinned. "You don't scare me, Saxon."

"That's 'cause you're too dumb to know I'm dangerous, babe. Leave the cuffs off. The lady isn't going anywhere."

Kurt waited until Patty left them alone and Dana sat down. "Let's go to work."

Gazing distantly, she lifted a shoulder. She made a soft snuffling sound. Kurt fished around inside his jacket and pulled out a large white handkerchief. He handed it over. Her full lips pulled into a faint grimace, but she took the handkerchief.

He poised his pen over the page. "What happened?"

She drew a deep, steadying breath and dabbed at her eyes with the handkerchief. "Well, I was in the middle of a conference with Pauline when those detectives invaded my office. They put handcuffs on me. Then they made me go downstairs with two police officers. I had to walk through the lobby—"

"Dana."

"What?"

"I'm not talking about today. I'm talking about Tuesday night. Tell me what happened."

"Nothing happened." A frown caused faint creases in her smooth forehead. "I was at home."

"You worked on Tuesday, right? What time did you go home?" He watched her closely. His clients lied to him, constantly and without fail. Some lied for self-protection, some lied because they were incapable of telling the truth, and some lied for the fun of it. Experience had taught him to listen and observe so he could winnow through the lies and find enough truth to help him in court. Yet, as he studied her fine features, large blue eyes and erect posture, a suspicion began to grow that he wouldn't hear any lies from this woman. He chewed over the novelty.

"I left work a little early. I suppose I got home around six."

Despite the edge of tear-induced roughness, her voice was dulcet toned, even musical. In it he heard confusion, indignation and fear, but not a trace of evasiveness. "You live with anyone?"

"No."

"Did you have company? Talk to anyone on the telephone? Chat with a neighbor?"

"I called my mother."

"What time did you call her?"

"I don't know. Seven-thirty?"

"How long did you talk?"

"I don't know." She pressed the handkerchief to her closed eyelids. "Not very long. My parents are vacationing in Hawaii and Mom was worried about the long-distance charges. Five minutes, perhaps, no longer than that."

Long distance calls he could confirm. "What about between nine-thirty and ten o'clock?"

She looked up at him. "I was in bed by then."

"Alone?"

"Yes, alone. Mr. Saxon, I did not kill anybody. I don't know why I'm here."

He heaved a heavy breath and tapped the pen on the table. Not much confused him, but this woman sure did. "Dana," he said, watching her eyes, "six witnesses picked you out of the lineup. Each one of them swears they saw you kill Eddie Gordon in the parking lot of O'Dooley's Bar and Grill.''

Her eyebrows reached heavenward.

Dana Benson blew him away. Her bewilderment was genuine—he'd stake his life on it.

More from curiosity than for any good reason, he shifted into a frontal assault. "One thing you got to learn fast is never lie to your attorney." He leaned forward, thrusting his jaw and scowling. "You want to confess you assassinated Kennedy, I won't blink. But you lie to me and I'm out of here."

Those big eyes got bigger and glittered with sapphire fury. "I *never* lie," she said, low and hateful.

He tapped the pen and his jaw worked, the muscles tightening in his cheeks. She was giving him "the look." Straight on, frosty, one eyebrow slightly raised, the other slightly lowered. A look telling him in no uncertain terms to go straight to hell, no detours. Only one look in a million could say so much without saying a word.

Thunderstruck, enchanted, he felt his heart rate speed to match the tempo of his tapping pen.

She pushed strands of moon-silver hair from her cheeks. "Obviously those witnesses are wrong. Do I look like the kind of person who would patronize a bar and grill?"

He dropped his foot to the floor and leaned over, giving her a long, pleasurable once-over, starting with her kidskin pumps. Her stocking-clad legs were long, slim and shapely, and the rest of her, attired in a light blue linen suit, was just as sweet.

He turned on the chair and jotted down a few notes. "Guess not. Sissy little juice bars are more your style."

Hot color rose in her cheeks. "I don't have to put up with this from you. I'd rather talk to Callister."

He repressed a smile. "You want somebody to take you to high tea, call Neal. But you're in a hell of a lot of trouble, and if you want out of it, you need me, lady."

"You're a bully."

"That's right."

"And you're rude."

"Give the lady a cigar."

She rubbed her eyes with the handkerchief. Tiny flakes of mascara drifted to her cheeks. "This is the stupidest situation I've ever been in, and you're not helping matters any."

"This isn't stupid, it's dead-on serious. So let's get to work."

First order of business, find an alibi. Taking copious notes, he had her go over everything she'd done on Tuesday night. Had she watched television? No. Why did she go to bed so early? She was tired. Could any of her neighbors vouch she'd been at home? She doubted it. She'd only moved into her home two months ago and didn't know her neighbors well. Besides, she lived at the end of a cul-de-sac and her house was very private.

Thoroughly disgusted, he scratched the back of his head and stared at his notes. "I can't believe you went to bed alone."

"That is not relevant."

Hearing how his comment had sounded, he lifted his shoulders. But he still couldn't believe it. The way he heard it, she and Neal Harlow were a hot item. Harlow must be a lot dopier than he looked if he let a beautiful woman like Dana sleep alone.

No matter how he looked at it, he couldn't see the possibility of an alibi. Six eyewitnesses were willing to state in court, under oath, they'd seen her kill a man. Could she be a psychopath? Insane? He sensed no mental instability. Besides, he trusted his instincts, and they said she was as innocent as a newborn kitten. "Okay, I'm going to do something I don't usually do, but these are desperate times. I'll allow Callister and Tannenbaum to interview you."

Her eyelids lowered and she turned her head, looking as if she'd rather have a truck run over her feet.

"You answer their questions," Kurt instructed her. "No elaboration. We want more information from them than they'll get from you. So if I tell you to shut you, you shut up. No arguments."

"It is not necessary for you to bark at me, Mr. Saxon." She rubbed her temples with her fingertips.

"I don't bark."

"Your tone of voice is completely unacceptable. I am neither stupid nor deaf."

Her cool formality made him feel light inside. He could listen to her voice for a hundred years and never tire of it. "Look, lady—"

"Don't call me *lady*, either."

"You're cranky." He nodded. "I understand."

She yelled, "I am not cranky!"

Yeah, and he bet she never lost her temper, either. "First let's get you something to eat. Sounds like you got a truck crawling around inside you." He slammed the briefcase shut. "It'll improve your attitude."

"My attitude? Your attitude is inexcusable. You came sweeping in here like some kind of dictator and, yes, you do too bark, Mr. Saxon! Talk, don't talk, shut up, sit down! Nobody talks to me like that. Nobody!" She clamped her arms over her chest. "And my bodily functions are of no concern to you, and if you had an ounce of decency you wouldn't mention them!"

She was giving him "the look" again, in spades. Calling her beautiful was like saying the ceiling in the Sistine Chapel was a nice piece of wall art. He wondered exactly how tight she and Neal were. Since Neal hadn't made an appearance, how close could they be? Mulling over the possibilities, he went to the door. "You want a burger?"

She stared at a watery blotch on the wall. "Fine." When he opened the door, she asked, "Do you believe me, Mr. Saxon?"

"I wouldn't be stupid enough to let you talk to the cops if I thought you were lying." He walked out of the room, wondering if, after he got her out on bail, she'd go out to dinner with him.

WHY KURT'S BACKHANDED admission of belief filled Dana with something akin to elation, she couldn't imagine. He was an awful man, rude, slovenly and unsympathetic. She disliked him intensely, and as soon as she made bail she'd most certainly take his advice and find another attorney. Not an attorney of Neal's choice, either.

Still, for now, knowing at least one person was on her side elevated her mood one hundred percent.

Kurt returned in a short time. He handed over a paper fast-food bag and a large soda. The hamburger was greasy, tasteless and salty; the french fries were limp. She devoured them, anyway. Kurt wrote on his pad, his concentration so intense she doubted if he knew she was in the room.

He directed her to sit at the end of the table. When Callister and Tannenbaum entered the room, Kurt placed his chair next to Dana's. It occurred to her that he positioned himself in such a way as to physically protect her. Ridiculous. Knight in shining armor he most definitely was not. His style was better befitting a barbarian at the gate.

Callister took her through the formalities again, having both her and Kurt sign a statement saying she'd agreed to this interview on the advice of counsel and that anything she said could be used against her in a court of law. The detective spoke into the tape recorder, stating the date and time, and he asked Dana to acknowledge her awareness about the interview being taped. She did so.

"All right." Callister sat on the table and folded his arms. "Tell us about Tuesday night."

Was that a question? She looked to Kurt. He lowered her eyelids slowly, telling her to go ahead. So she told them exactly what she'd told Kurt.

It didn't take a genius to know neither detective believed a word. It appalled her, and made her more than a little angry. No one had ever doubted her word before.

"I think you're failing to grasp the situation," Tannenbaum said mildly. "We know you were at O'Dooley's on Tuesday night. The bartender remembers you. People in the parking lot remember you. A couple of waitresses fooling around with a video camera took a movie of you."

Her mouth dropped open.

Kurt held up a hand. "Call her a liar again and this interview is over."

Tannenbaum locked gazes with Kurt. The attorney didn't make a sound; his icy glare spoke for him. The detective looked away first.

Kurt's control of the situation struck a chord of response deep within Dana. He believed in her, and because he did, he'd fight—figuratively—to the death on her behalf. Callister's hostility didn't cow him. Tannenbaum's deceptively soft demeanor and the bulldog determination in his eyes didn't make him falter. If Kurt could stand up to them, she certainly could. She sat taller on the chair.

Callister placed an eight-by-ten color photograph in front of Dana. "Okay, then let's talk about Gordon."

Dana studied the photograph of a man. It showed his shoulders and head, but he didn't look quite real. His skin was waxy and gray; his half-closed eyes were dull, sunken into the sockets. Something pinkish stained the corners of his mouth. A soft drink perhaps, or...blood.

He was dead! She gasped and clapped a hand over her mouth.

Kurt flipped over the photograph and shoved it across the table. "This is an interview, not show-and-tell. No pictures."

"Who is he to you, Dana?" Callister rested his lanky weight on both hands planted flat on the table-top. "Is he your dope dealer?"

"I've never seen him before."

"Then why did you shoot him?"

The laughter came from nowhere, bubbling up inside. Attempts to repress it gave her a stomachache. Finally she turned on the chair. Bent so her chin nearly touched her knee, she swallowed the paroxysms of hysteria. If she laughed, they'd lock her up for certain.

"Hey," Callister said, "no puking in here."

"I'm...not...sick," she choked out, gaining some control. She wiped her eyes with the handkerchief. "Mr. Callister, if you possessed even a modicum of common sense you would realize that is the stupidest thing anyone has ever said to me. Shoot somebody? Me? You are out of your mind."

Kurt made a strangled noise into his fist. His eyes sparkled. His approval touched her and put steel in her spine.

"How do you account for all the people who saw you?"

"Either they're lying or they're sorely mistaken. I've never even been to that O'Dooley place."

Tannenbaum produced a small sheet of paper enclosed in a waxy, transparent sleeve. He laid it in front of her. "Ever seen this before?"

She studied the paper for several seconds before she realized it was a page from her desk calendar. In her handwriting were the words *O'Dooley's, Brewer Street, 9:00.*

All sense of triumph fled. "That woman!" Full of apology, she gave Kurt a helpless look. "I forgot. A woman asked to meet me at O'Dooley's."

Kurt half turned on the chair to face her. "Who is she?"

"I don't know." She racked her memory. "Sometime Monday, I don't know when exactly, she called me at work. My assistant will know. She took the call initially."

"Got a name?" Callister asked.

"She wouldn't give me a name. I didn't go to O'Dooley's."

"Uh-huh." Callister was openly skeptical.

"It's true! She did call me and she did ask to meet me at the bar. I don't know who she is or why she called. Maybe she looks like me. And—and there was a big story in the paper yesterday. My picture was in there. People must have seen it and confused us."

"You've got an evil twin. Sure. Let's go over it again. What is your relationship to Eddie Gordon—"

Kurt's chair scraped the tile and he stood. "That's it. Interview over. Miss Benson, don't say another word."

"Now, hold on a minute, Saxon." Tannenbaum held up a placating hand. "Let's not be hasty."

"I want the names of those witnesses and a copy of the videotape."

Callister's dour face turned thunderous. "File a motion, counselor."

Kurt snarled a string of scatological verbiage that made Dana sink lower in the chair. Callister replied in kind, moving in until he was nearly nose-to-nose with the attorney. He and Kurt were the same height, but Kurt out-bulked him, and, to Dana's mortified fascination, his vocabulary was far more colorful than the detective's. In spite of herself, she was impressed.

Callister stalked out of the room. He slammed the door.

"I got that on tape, Saxon." Tannenbaum patted the recorder. His hound dog eyes filled with sorrowful reproach.

"Get this, too. I told you not to call her a liar and you did, so you blew the interview."

Once again alone with Kurt, Dana buried her face in her hands and rocked on the chair. "This is awful! Why did you do that? You made them so angry. I'll never get out of here."

"It went great. They can't shake you and they know it." He piled papers into the briefcase. "What do you remember about that woman?"

That was his idea of going great? She supposed he considered tornadoes mere breezes. "There's nothing to remember. She called. I forgot about it. It was a very short conversation. Did the interview really go well?"

"Better than that. They need a confession. It tells me the physical evidence is weak."

"I don't understand. All those witnesses . . ."

"Let me worry about the witnesses. You worry about the woman who called. Think about it. Try to remember details."

"I'll try. Can I go home now?"

He checked his watch. "In a bit. You have to go before the judge." He patted his briefcase. "Bail will be no sweat."

Hugging her elbows, she shivered. The strange phone call from the strange woman acquired a sinister cast. What might have happened if she'd taken the request seriously and actually gone to O'Dooley's? "I swear I did not kill anybody. I've never been to O'Dooley's, and I can't imagine why everyone is saying I was there."

"It's mistaken identity. It happens more often than anybody likes to admit. Lawyers know it." He raked hair off his forehead. "Unfortunately, juries love eyewitnesses. We're talking high drama." He drew back his shoulders and pointed at his reflection in the mirror. "'That's him!' Just like they see on television. What a load of crap."

After the masterful way he'd handled the detectives, she regarded his theatrics in a more forgiving light. He might be rude and crude, but he certainly seemed to know how to get what he wanted.

"Memory is a screwball thing. You say your picture was in the paper?"

"Yesterday. The *Morning News* business section."

"Good likeness?"

She'd liked the photograph, but was a poor judge of how much it resembled her. "I suppose so."

He smiled. Not a big smile nor a particularly happy smile. It softened his eyes, though, and made Dana concede, grudgingly, that perhaps he wasn't totally hideous. He had large, even features and a muscular jaw. His hair was overdue for a trimming, but it was thick and a dark, rich brown. His pale eyes were lively and quick, compelling in their contrast with his dark suntan. If he weren't so rough looking, she supposed some might call him passably not bad looking.

"Our biggest problem right now is finding out who the prosecutor is and what he's going to charge you with."

"I thought they said murder."

He picked up the photograph of the victim. Holding it so she couldn't see, he studied it. "Scuttlebutt says first-degree, but I don't believe it. We'll prepare for the worst, though. Are you sure you have no idea who this guy is?"

She lowered her eyelids, praying he wouldn't make her look at that awful picture again. "I've never seen him before."

"Whatever. Right now, I have to run down some information. Can Neal get into your bank accounts for the bail?"

"Pauline can. She's my business partner."

The door opened and Patty poked her head inside. "I need to take your client, Saxon." She dangled a pair of handcuffs.

Dana closed her eyes and braced herself for the cold humiliation of the iron bracelets on her wrists. A heavy hand on her shoulder made her open her eyes.

Kurt smiled, reassuring and strong. He gave her shoulder a squeeze. "You've got guts you don't know about. You'll be all right."

Crudely put, but it served to remind her that she was a fighter. The police and those witnesses were lying about her. Lies were the one thing she could not, would not, tolerate.

"We'll beat this, Dana."

She lifted her head higher. This was unjust. She knew it. Kurt Saxon knew it. By the time this was over, the police would know it, too. The handcuffs no longer embarrassed her. "Yes, Mr. Saxon, we most certainly will."

Chapter Four

"We've got problems," Kurt said.

Dana clutched her purse to her breast as she followed the attorney out of the police station. "We don't have problems. They turned me loose. And I thank you from the depths of my heart."

"For now."

"You'd rather I went to jail?"

When they reached the doors, he instructed her to tie her scarf over her hair. He slipped a pair of dark sunglasses on her face.

She pushed his hands away. "The sun is almost down. Why—?"

"Reporters. Most of them are probably waiting over at the courthouse to see what kind of bail you get, but some wise guy always hears about a release before everyone else."

He had to be kidding. She searched his face. He wasn't kidding. She hadn't thought about the press or what might happen when her name hit the newspapers. What would her friends think? Or worse, what about her clients, who trusted Star Systems to store their valuable computer data based upon her reputation for security, honesty and confidentiality? It finally came home to her that walking out these doors didn't mean her nightmare was ending, but that it had barely begun.

She tied the silk scarf over her hair. "Why me? I didn't do anything. The police let me go. They know I didn't do it."

"We Texans love a good scandal," he drawled with a grin. Wrapping a brawny arm around her shoulders, he straight-armed through the double doors.

A man with a camera yelled, "Here she is!"

Down the street, a dark-haired woman broke into a jog. The camera light flared, momentarily blinding Dana despite the dark glasses. Keeping a tight grip on her shoulders, Kurt raised his other arm in an unmistakable threat. The camera man yelped and scurried backward.

Kurt hustled her to a car. Dana had only seconds to absorb the sight of a boat-sized black Lincoln Continental before Kurt all but shoved her inside.

The dark-haired woman caught up to them. For a moment she bent at the waist, gulping in air. "I'm Trudy—"

Kurt turned on the reporter. "No comments, no interviews."

"Is it true the police dropped the arrest warrant? Does that mean your client has been cleared as a suspect?"

Dana watched in awe as the petite reporter clung to Kurt's heels like a yappy little dog, shouting questions until he reached the driver's side and got in. He locked the doors.

When he drove off, headed for Highway 75 north, Dana tore off the sunglasses and untied the scarf. The floorboard at her feet was littered with folders, a baseball glove, books and electrical cords. The car smelled funny, too, vaguely rank, like wet charcoal. She gingerly pushed debris aside with the toe of her shoe. The back seat was filled with clothing, boxes and books.

As if she'd asked, Kurt said, "I lost my apartment. The goof next door was smoking in bed and set the whole place on fire. The entire building was condemned. Haven't had time to find a place, so I've been sacking out at my office."

"Oh. I'm very sorry."

He shot her a grin. "It was a cruddy place, anyway."

She wondered why he'd been living in a cruddy place. She'd thought attorneys made good money. He made her curious, but curiosity had no place in their increasingly odd relationship. She suspected the less she knew, the better she'd feel. So she returned to the subject of reporters. "We should talk to the press. I'm innocent. I should tell them my side of the story and how it's all a big mistake."

"My rule, no reporters."

He slouched nonchalantly on the seat and steered with one hand draped lazily over the steering wheel. A thumping rock-and-roll tune played on the radio, and he kept time with his restless fingers. "Fact of life, babe, innocence makes lousy copy. They look at you and all they see is a good girl gone bad. Along with dollar signs, of course.''

"That's absurd. I haven't gone bad. I've never done anything bad in my life.''

He steered the big car onto the highway and picked up speed. The car began to vibrate and make a rattling noise. "I know it and you know it. Until the state of Texas realizes it, etch this onto your brain cells. The press is the enemy.''

The cold conviction of his words made protests die in her throat.

"Like I was saying before, we got problems.''

"I'm free.'' A headache throbbed in her temples. The stinking, rattletrap old car, sounding as if it had severe intestinal problems, wasn't helping any.

"For now. Them dropping the arrest warrant means they need a confession.''

"I won't confess. I didn't do it.''

"I hope like hell you've never owned a gun.''

"I don't have a gun. I've never had a gun. I thought you believed me, Mr. Saxon.''

"I do. And call me Kurt.'' He flashed a grin. "Because they released you doesn't mean you're cleared. Not by a long shot. You're still their prime suspect. All those witnesses placed you at the scene. What I'm thinking is nobody witnessed the actual shooting. Trouble is, unless they formally charge you, I can't find out what kind of evidence they have.''

"There is no evidence.''

"Not yet.''

That was not what Dana wanted to hear. She stared out the window at the bumper-to-bumper traffic. Under normal circumstances, Kurt's fast driving and weaving in and out of traffic would panic her. At the moment she was too tired to care. All she wanted to do was go home.

"Problem number one is the lineup. Six witnesses, no hesitations, no maybes."

"That's not possible," she murmured. Knowing six strangers were lying about her shook her to the core. She noticed her reflection in the window glass. The very idea of a murderer, wearing her face, running around loose in Dallas, was beyond comprehension. So why were all those people lying about her? "Can we talk to the witnesses? If they see me face-to-face, they'll realize their mistake."

"Callister and Tannenbaum are a bigger concern. They're good cops, cautious. They picked you up because of the witnesses, put you through the lineup, got their ID. Then they let you go. I know they executed a search warrant, so that tells us they didn't find anything. No weapon, no dope, no connection to Eddie Gordon—"

"Wait a minute! Dope? Do you mean drugs?"

"Eddie Gordon was a two-bit dealer. A hustler with a long string of arrests. So the cops think you're slumming. Picking up a little nose-candy, and the deal went sour so you shot your dealer. Fact of life, prosecutors love well-to-do hoity-toity types who dabble their toes in scummy water. These kind of cases are great for political careers and scoring points. They'll be after you in the worst kind of way."

"None of this is making any sense."

"A lot of things don't make sense. That's why we're going to make an aggressive defense. No sitting around waiting to see if they make another arrest. Because trust me, if they arrest you again, they will make it stick."

"You are scaring me." She sank lower in the seat. She didn't want to hear this. She didn't even like action-adventure movies or cop shows on television.

"Relax, you got me." He gunned the engine, and the big car shot in front of a semitrailer. "I sure would like to get my hands on that videotape."

She sagged even lower. "I forgot about that."

"Don't sweat it." He laughed. "It can't be any good. The film was shot at night, outdoors. The quality has to be poor. I'm thinking the murderer might have your coloring. Similar, but not exact. Then your picture shows up in the paper the day after the shooting. Very convenient. One guy sees the picture, it's pretty close, so he talks to the other witnesses and they all say, yeah, that's her. I'll bet they mentioned the video as a scare tactic, trying to pressure you."

"Then you're saying this isn't hopeless?"

He dropped his hand atop hers and squeezed her fingers. "Hey, we have problems, babe, but nothing is ever hopeless. Not with me around."

She pulled her hand away from his. "Please do not call me babe, Mr. Saxon."

She glumly watched the heavy traffic. The streetlights flashed pinkish gold across the side window. Usually she adored the city at night with its art deco skyline and vibrancy. Now the traffic noise worsened her headache, and the constant activity made her all the more anxious to reach the peace and quiet of home.

After a mile or so, Kurt said, "You are one."

"One what?" Something about his grin made her regret responding. He was about to annoy her. She could feel it.

"A babe. See, I've always had this fantasy." He waved a hand in a slow arc. "Picture it. I'm in my office, growling about the usual garbage, then *she* walks in. She's tall and slim, her blond hair smooth as silk, smooth as her voice. Everything from the way she dresses to the look in her eyes is pure class." He caught her dumbfounded expression and laughed. "She says, 'Kurt, I need you. Save me.' So I do, and we live happily ever after."

She crossed her arms. She'd asked for an attorney and got a six-feet-four-inch Groucho Marx. "You are the oddest man I have ever met."

"What? You don't want to be my fantasy girl?"

His cocky impudence made anger impossible. She had to fight a smile. "I appreciate the attempt to cheer me up, but I'm really too tired for jokes."

"You have to be hungry. I'll buy you dinner."

"No, thank you."

"Take your mind off your problems. Besides, we still have work to do."

"No, we don't have work to do. I appreciate you taking the time to drive me home, but the only thing I'm doing is taking a hot shower, having a stiff drink and then going to bed."

"Alone?"

"Mr. Saxon!"

He winced, but he didn't look the least bit repentant. "Just asking. You're my client. I'm duty-bound to keep tabs on you. Besides, there might be reporters waiting for you."

She dropped her face into her hands. "At my house?" she asked with a groan. "They have to leave me alone."

"You're hot news. A society girl. Nothing makes a reporter happier than to see someone like you take a pratfall."

He made her sound like a caricature with nothing better to do than play tennis while drinking margaritas. "I am not a society girl. I'm a businesswoman. I work very hard."

His pale gaze slanted toward her. A little shock pinged her when she realized he wasn't teasing her or making a joke. His blunt speech simply called the shots as he saw them. Rumpled suit and shimmying, litter-filled automobile aside, this man knew what he talked about. The realization didn't make her feel better.

"If you were some hooker or habitual check-kiter, no big deal. Nobody cares. But a nice lady from a good family, under suspicion in a shooting, is a sure bet for front-page coverage. The cops will let it slip you're the prime suspect, so reporters will go scurrying around, talking to your neighbors and family. They'll find people you went to school with."

"But they let me go."

"Hey, every crime reporter's fantasy is to break a big case before the cops do."

"What about...?" Her tight throat made her squeak. She cleared it. "Do you think they'll go to Star Systems?" She rubbed her fist between her breasts. Breathing hurt. Star Systems Data Storage had clients who considered their mailing lists and industrial data as confidential as state secrets. She and Pauline based their reputation on offering secure storage. No matter how this turned out, it was going to hurt.

They rode in silence until Kurt reached her neighborhood and turned down her street. "Well, hell," he drawled, echoing her sentiments exactly. "Sometimes I hate being right. Reconsider dinner, Dana."

She recognized Pauline's Mustang parked in her driveway. Emotion added to the tightness in her chest. Despite their recent problems, Pauline was the best friend anyone could ever hope for. "It's okay, she's not a reporter."

Kurt pulled into the driveway next to Pauline's car.

Pauline hurried to Dana's side and they embraced. "I've been waiting and waiting. Neal said you didn't go to jail, but he didn't know where you were. Are you okay? You look like hell." She stepped back and critically eyed Dana's face. "You been crying?"

"I'm okay. The police turned me loose. Pauline, this is Kurt Saxon. He's an attorney. Mr. Saxon, my partner, Pauline Kidder."

The redhead stepped back and looked Kurt over from head to toe. "Good gawd, but you're a big fella. I bet you work out."

Shaking her head, Dana dug out her keys and headed for the front door.

She felt it as soon as she entered the house. Her home had been invaded. Disbelief growing, she walked through the rooms, noting the opened drawers, loose cushions on furniture and general disarray. She paused at a plant shelf and ran a hand over the wood. She stared at the black, greasy smudges on her fingertips.

"Fingerprint powder." Kurt shoved his hands in his trouser pockets and rocked on his heels.

"It looks like soot. What were they thinking?" Powder stained the champagne-colored carpeting and the walls. "It's disgusting."

"You ought to sue," Pauline said. Hands on her hips, her mouth hanging open, she studied the damage. "This is sick. Just plain sick. They can't get away with this."

Dana stalked toward the kitchen. The kitchen was in bad shape, too. Drawers and cabinets hung open. Pots and pans littered the floor. She whirled on her attorney. "Can't they show a little common decency and respect for my property?"

Kurt lifted his shoulders and showed her the palms of his hands.

Some help you are, she thought sourly. She flung her purse on the breakfast counter.

She started a pot of coffee. The simple chore soothed her: fill the carafe with cold water, fit a filter into the basket, measure the coffee. She was free, away from the noise, smells, hostility, mean-eyed stares and confusion. Her temper cooled, but the anxiety rested in her belly like a nervous little animal, ready to snap.

"What happens next, Mr. Saxon?"

"First, you call me Kurt. Second, don't be so chintzy with the coffee. I like mine strong."

She'd almost forgotten her initial assessment of his character. Now she remembered he was rude and demanding. And big. Despite vaulted ceilings and oversize windows, the house seemed too small to contain him. From the corner of her eye, she watched Pauline slide onto a bar stool. She smiled sweetly at Kurt, and her eyes were bright with interest.

Dana added an extra scoop of coffee.

Pauline rested her chin on the back of her hands. "So what happens next, Kurt? Is she going on trial for murder?"

Good heavens, Dana thought in disgust. Pauline was flirting with the man. Worse, he responded. His smile widened and his posture turned jaunty. "Did the police talk to you?"

Uncertainly, Pauline drew back. "They kept asking me about some guy named Eddie Gordon. Hell, I don't know him. They were asking everybody the same thing. Who is he?"

"Did they talk to you about Dana?" He brought out a pen and a tattered little notebook. He flipped to a clean page. "What specific questions did they ask?"

Looking miffed, Pauline crossed her arms. Men usually gave her exactly what she wanted, when she wanted it. Kurt must be a new experience for her, Dana mused.

Dana puttered aimlessly around the kitchen. She hated herself for thinking it, but Pauline sounded ghoulish, acting as if the excitement were some kind of adventure. The arrest and lineup and interrogation had been horrible. Dana had never felt so helpless and afraid in her life.

"You look worn out, Dana," Kurt said. "Hit the showers and get comfortable. I'll fix some chow."

Her stretched-tight nerves frayed. Her vision blurred. "You are my attorney, not my keeper. Stop ordering me around." She sagged against the counter and clutched her midsection. Control was slipping away from her, and that, more than the police, frightened her. Shaking began in her knees and worked its way up and around, until she shivered so hard her teeth chattered. "Stop bar-barking at me."

Pauline stiffened. "Dana?"

She couldn't stop shaking. The tighter she hugged herself, the harder she tensed her muscles, the worse she shivered. Fresh terror gripped her. She was breaking down. At any moment she'd collapse in a lump, burst into tears and wail.

Kurt patted her shoulder. "Hey, hey, I don't bark," he said. "I'm a cat person."

The inanity of his comment caught her attention. She lifted her face and found his gray eyes dark with concern. The shivering eased. She whispered, "What did you say?"

"Dogs are too subservient." His large hand slowed so that he stroked instead of patted her arm. "Of course, can't take a cat jogging, but that's the only real drawback."

Unable to decide if he was talking nonsense to distract her or if in some bizarre manner he was making fun of her, she blinked slowly.

His mouth pulled into a crooked grin. "Have to admire a ten-pound critter who feels absolutely certain, if he wanted to, he could take me." He squeezed her upper arm. "You like cats?"

"I . . . suppose."

He eased a tendril of hair off her cheek. The intimate feel of his fingers on her face caused a catch in her throat. Awareness of his size struck her anew. At five-foot-nine, she was as tall or taller than most men she knew, but Kurt Saxon made her feel petite. Suddenly, she wanted nothing more than to fall into his embrace. She wanted those big arms holding her tightly, protecting her from the nightmare. She wanted to feel his warmth against her cheek and listen to his heart and have him pet her and tell her everything would be all right.

If Pauline weren't standing there all wide-eyed and worried, Dana might have done exactly that.

Stooping so low as to want physical comfort from this hulking brute appalled her. He wasn't the least bit appealing, not in any way, shape or form. She didn't need his comfort and she certainly didn't want it.

"Are you okay?" Pauline eased around the counter and touched Dana's hand with tentative fingers. "It's weird seeing you lose it." To Kurt, she added, "Usually she's so laid-back, nothing bugs her. You know, don't worry, be happy, and all that rot."

Thoroughly embarrassed, Dana stepped away from both of them. "I just need a shower." She went upstairs.

She stayed in the shower a long time, soaping herself over and over, shampooing her hair three times, trying to wash the stink of the police station out of her memory. It helped bring back her equilibrium. Her little breakdown had been a delayed stress reaction, that's all. She wasn't losing her mind.

When she finished, she found Pauline awaiting her in the bedroom.

"You okay, hon?" Seated on the bed, Pauline toyed with a pillow shaped like a large satin rose. Her expression was a mixture of concern and wary curiosity.

"I'm okay now." She dressed in a blue fleece jogging suit and flopped onto the bed next to her friend. "I know it's all a big mistake, but I am still so scared. I can't believe this is happening."

Pauline swatted her playfully with the pillow. "Hey, at least you have Kurt." She rolled her eyes. "What a gorgeous side of beef! Is he a friend of Neal's? You ever met him before? Have you been holding out on me?"

Dana eyed the ceiling. "You are incredible."

"I know." Pauline patted her curly mop. "He asked for my phone number. Good gawd, I haven't seen such a beautiful head of hair in all my life. You could drown in it. And those eyes! He's so intense. You don't think he's married, do you?"

"I don't know. Furthermore, I don't care." Dana jumped to her feet. "Why is it I always forget how impossible you are? Are you going to help or drool over my attorney?"

"Can't I do both?" her partner asked with a saucy grin. "Come on, lighten up." She lifted her shoulders in a quick shrug. "I can give you an alibi if you want.

What's the big deal? I'll say we went to dinner or something."

This was typical of Pauline: her problems were cause for declaring a national emergency; other peoples' problems called for jokes. "I don't need an alibi. I didn't hurt anybody." She aimlessly wandered around the bedroom, trailing her fingers over the marble fireplace mantel and fingering framed photographs of her parents. How was she going to tell them she was a prime suspect in a murder? The worst news she'd ever had to give them was that she'd flopped on a test or had a fender bender with the family car.

"I don't see how one little white lie can hurt. We've got a business to think about, you know." Pauline tossed the pillow behind her and rose, smoothing her short black skirt. "With this kind of publicity, we might as well just shut our doors and go get jobs at McDonald's. We were lucky as hell no clients saw the arrest. I'm not risking Star Systems over crap like this."

Hurt slithered through Dana and her eyes began to burn. She understood what Pauline meant, but even so...

"I talked to Kurt while you were in the shower. He says you'll need time for the legal wheeling and dealing. I think that's a good idea. You need a vacation, anyway. I can handle things. You can do a lot of work at home." She jerked a thumb toward the computer on the desk in the corner of the bedroom. "Shoot, you can modem or fax just about everything. There's no need for you to come in at all."

Facing the fireplace, fearing if she turned around that she'd begin to cry, Dana nodded. "If we're really lucky, we won't lose any accounts."

For several long, ticking seconds, Pauline remained silent. When she spoke, her voice was low and strained. "That isn't what I meant."

Right.

"I mean it, Dana. I'm here, right? Moral support and all that rot. I'm behind you a hundred percent."

Too much eagerness colored Pauline's words. Dana drew several deep breaths and forced a smile before she turned around. She honestly did understand. Part of her felt the same way as Pauline did. They'd both sunk everything into Star Systems. They'd made sacrifices in money, time, energy and in their personal lives. One person didn't—couldn't—matter as much as the business.

Understanding didn't lessen the hurt one little bit.

"I'll take a couple days off."

Pauline fiddled with the doorknob. "I really think it'll be for the best." She opened the door, then added, "For you. The best for you."

Dana bit back the urge to argue. Especially as another, more sinister, thought crept darkly into her brain. Did Pauline think she was guilty? "But, no lies. No alibis. I have nothing to hide."

As they walked down the curved staircase, Dana couldn't make herself look at Pauline. Her friend had a hard edge to her, a sharp selfishness that bordered on ruthlessness. What Pauline wanted, Pauline got, the world be damned. Under other circumstances, Dana admired Pauline's often ferocious determination. She saw now with depressing clarity that if Pauline had to choose between friendship and Star Systems, friendship would lose.

When they reached the foyer, Dana studied the black gunk on her hand. Fingerprint powder coated the banister.

"Do you think the cops found anything?" Pauline asked.

Like what? she almost asked, but caught herself in time. "Did they do this to the office, too?"

"They were all over the place. They took some files and bank statements and a bunch of stuff out of your desk. Why'd they want bank statements?"

"I haven't the faintest idea."

"You'd best get this straightened out. And fast." She turned her wrist and glanced at her watch. "I better go. I have a, uh—"

"You have a date. It's okay. I'm all right. I appreciate you being here for me." She was glad Pauline had an excuse to leave. "I'll let you know if there's any news."

"Say goodbye to Kurt for me." She flashed a broad smile, but it didn't reach her eyes. "And find out if he's married."

"Sure." She saw Pauline out.

Dana locked the front door, then rested her forehead against the cool wood.

A disheartening feeling said their past arguments would seem like petty squabbles by the time this was over.

Chapter Five

The smell of food drew Dana to the kitchen.

Kurt stood in front of the range. He had removed his jacket and tie and rolled his shirt sleeves to reveal corded forearms. Cowboys and construction workers had muscles like that, she thought, trying to rouse disdain.

She failed.

You are such a snob, she chided herself. All her life she'd had to be on guard against people who tried to pigeonhole her as a dumb blonde or just another pretty face. Here she was judging him on his appearance.

Besides, watching him handle a spatula like a master chef while supple muscles flexed under his shirt roused anything but disdain. And he did have nice hair. Thick and shaggy, in need of a trim, it curled at the ends where it fell over his collar.

His looks didn't matter. What did matter was the kindness underlying his gruff exterior. His belief in her innocence mattered. Especially after the way Pauline had revealed her true concerns.

He poured a mug of coffee and plopped it on the breakfast counter. "I've seen college kids with better-stocked kitchens. Sit."

She noticed the sink was full of soapy water and he'd done a fair job of wiping fingerprint powder off the counters. He'd also closed drawers and cabinets. "I like to bake, but I'm not much of a day-to-day cook."

"I can tell." With a flourish worthy of a television show chef, he slid an omelet onto a plate. "Lucky for you, I'm inventive." He set the omelet and a salad in front of her. "Do you have a padlock for the back gate? You don't need reporters or thrill-seekers peeking in your windows."

She tossed a nervous glance at the French doors leading to her tiny backyard. If she ever caught anyone peeking in her windows, she'd have a heart attack. "I'll find one. Do you cook for all your clients?"

"Only the really beautiful ones." He saluted her with his coffee mug. "Did Pauline leave?"

His warm smile gave her the disconcerting feeling that he actually thought she was beautiful. She focused on the omelet. She shouldn't be wondering if he'd taken Pauline's number because of the murder case or if he meant to ask her out. She shouldn't care. "She had a date. What happens next?"

"Your number one job right now is remembering Tuesday. And I do mean remember. Everything, everyone you talked to, every place you went, every detail." He nudged a sheet of paper closer to her. "I made a list of things for you to do. Be thorough. No detail is too small or insignificant."

He frowned at his wristwatch. "I have some things to do. Is there anyone who can stay with you tonight?" He nodded at the telephone answering machine. "Screen phone calls?"

"I can take care of myself."

Kurt looked skeptical. "Turn off the telephone and let the machine answer. These things always bring out the cranks. No need to let them upset you. Ignore anybody at the door. I'll be back in the morning." He searched inside his jacket and brought out a business card which he laid on the counter. He slung the jacket over his shoulder.

"You're quite a take-charge kind of man."

"That's my style." Moving next to her, he grazed her chin with a gentle knuckle. "We'll fight this thing, Dana. We'll win."

He looked past her to the glass-fronted bookcase where she displayed her collection of folk and fairy tales. "Do you believe in fairy tales?"

Abashed to have him notice her childish interest, she smiled. "I've been collecting those books all my life. Some are quite old."

"Cute hobby." His gaze roamed. All through the house, her passion for fairy tales was evident in figurines of knights, princesses and wee folk, reproductions of old tapestries and cartoon character dolls. "You can consider me your white knight, then. Shield up, sword drawn. I've already made up my mind. You'll walk away from this."

She believed him—trusted him with all her heart. After that tense little scene with Pauline, she desperately needed someone to believe in. Someone who believed in her. "Thank you." The words emerged in a husky whisper.

His suntanned skin formed a shadow under his white shirt, and veins rose like cords on the back of his hand as he held his jacket. She sensed he was inches away from touching her. From stroking her hair, perhaps, or cupping his big hand against her cheek.

And she would welcome it. She repeated, "Thank you . . . Kurt."

Looking satisfied, he moved away. She had slid off the stool to see him out when he stopped and looked over his shoulder. "You're dating Neal Harlow."

He gave her the distinct impression that whether or not she dated Neal didn't matter to him. He was interested, and he wasn't the type to allow an interest to wither.

Caught off guard, she toyed with the hem of her sweatshirt. "We used to date. We don't see much of each other anymore."

Light filled his strange, pale eyes and they gleamed, accentuating his suddenly boyish smile. Dana's breath caught in her throat and her heart skipped a beat. His eyes trapped her, held her fast, drowned her in pure intensity. His aggressively male posture and glowing smile offered a promise that made her mouth turn dry.

As she closed the door behind him and locked it, she heard him whistling as he strolled toward his car.

Her back to the door, slightly breathless, she thought at least Kurt Saxon gave her something besides the police to think about.

DANA LOOKED THROUGH the peephole in the front door. Neal Harlow stood on her porch. He pressed the bell again, and the soft chime echoed in the foyer. She debated whether or not to follow Kurt Saxon's instructions to the letter. Yesterday had been pure hell, and Neal had refused to come to the police station.

Still, what could he have done?

She opened the door.

As usual, he wore an Italian suit over a crisply starched shirt and silk tie. His wingtip shoes gleamed with a hard shine. His up and down perusal, taking in her sweatsuit, rubber gloves, hair piled messily on her head and makeup-free face, made her regret answering the door. She hated Neal seeing her looking like this. She hated sensing his disapproval. Around him, she always felt an overwhelming need to look her best with her hair fixed, makeup perfect and her clothing impeccable. How was it she ever imagined she could love this man?

"May I come in?"

"The house is a mess. I'm cleaning." She stripped off the rubber gloves. "But come on in."

The air was heavy with the scents of lemon cleanser and bleach. The fingerprint powder had proved as messy and nasty as soot. Even so, cleaning it off the furniture and walls hadn't been nearly as bad as returning her house to order. The police had searched her house from top to bottom—she'd even found evidence where they'd lifted the tops off the toilet tanks. Imagining them pawing through her underwear made her ill.

"I was worried about you," the attorney said. "Is everything all right?"

She laughed dryly. She picked up a bucket and mop and headed for the kitchen. "I'm the prime suspect in the murder of a drug dealer. Other than that, life is just ducky. Would you like a cup of coffee?"

"Is Kurt here?"

"And that's another thing." She gave him a cup of coffee along with cream and sugar. "Where did you find him? He's a flesh-and-blood bulldozer." She dumped the bucket of dirty water, then stared out the window over the sink. Thunderclouds built on the horizon. "Why didn't you come to the police station yesterday? I needed a friend."

"I'm a corporate attorney. There's nothing I could have done for you. I know Kurt is a little... intimidating, but he's good. As soon as I heard about the evidence the police have against you, I knew Kurt was exactly the attorney you needed."

"Evidence against...?" Dana ran water over the mop head and squeezed it extra hard. "Do you think I killed that man?"

Neal sat on a stool and began dressing his coffee with precisely measured doses of cream and sugar.

Her forehead tightened. Neal was as fussy about his coffee as he was about his clothing, but she sensed he was stalling. She heard the unspoken question: Did you do it, Dana? Was he speculating about how she may have gone temporarily insane, or if she had a secret drug problem, or if she was living a double life that included guns and smoky bars?

She wished she'd followed Kurt's advice and hadn't answered the door.

"Dana, I know Kurt is not the type of person you generally deal with. But I know about your financial situation and how your assets are tied up in the business. Most attorneys would ask for thousands of dollars up front. Criminal defense can be very expensive. Kurt isn't cheap, but he is reasonable. You might say he has a bit of a Quixote complex." He made it sound like a character flaw.

"Lovely, but I wasn't talking about Kurt. I asked you a question." Shut up, she told herself. You're setting yourself up for hurt feelings. "Do you think I killed that man?"

Neal eased the back of one hand over his forehead, smoothing sandy hair into place. He sipped the coffee. "I would never presume to ask you about guilt or innocence. That is not my place or my concern. I do advise that you not discuss the case with me. Since I'm not your attorney on record, I could be subpoenaed as a witness. In fact, in light of our history, I probably will be."

She dropped the mop into the bucket. It clattered. She turned her head slowly to face him. His eyebrows twitched and his slightly prominent Adam's apple bobbed. "What," she said softly, "is that supposed to mean?"

"I mean, you shouldn't be discussing case particulars with anyone except your attorney."

She laughed and swung her head side to side. "You think I did it." She tried to see his eyes, but he was finding his shirt cuff of great interest. "You actually think I killed somebody. Or is it, you're glad I'm in trouble?''

"That's a horrible thing to say. Not to mention unfair," he protested, but his face reddened and he looked everywhere except at her. "I came over here with a purpose. If you're going to be unreasonable, then perhaps I should limit my contacts to your attorney."

Curiosity overrode her anger. She picked up a sponge and attacked the cabinet fronts. "What purpose?"

"You saw the newspaper this morning."

Her throat tightened. Along with a large photograph of her slinking out through the lobby looking ashamed and guilty, a front-page story had announced her arrest. "I saw it."

"They said the man was shot."

Dana paused in her scrubbing. "I didn't shoot anybody."

"I'm not saying you did." He tapped a spoon against the coffee cup.

"I've never owned a gun. I've never even touched one."

"I used to."

She peered closely at him. A muscle jumped in his cheek and he lowered his eyelids, bracing them as if in protection from a sand-filled wind. A bad feeling spread through her chest. "So?"

"It's gone." He took a hurried sip of coffee. He still wouldn't look at her. "The last time I actually recall seeing it was around New Year's, but it's gone now."

He glanced at her, a furtive little dart of his eyes. "Guns are easily traced. Mine is registered in my name."

She considered what he was saying. As his meaning sank in, she clenched the sponge so tightly water dribbled onto the floor. "I get it, you think I'm not only a killer, but a thief, as well."

"I am not accusing you of anything."

"That's exactly what you're doing. How could you? How *dare* you?"

"I am not accusing you! I merely find it fair to warn you..." His eyes glazed and his chin actually quivered. The vulnerable expression passed quickly. His face turned hard. He held his thumb and forefinger half an inch apart. "I'm this close to making full partner in the firm, Dana. I've worked my tail off to get where I am today. You know how much it means to me. I can't afford any connection to the murder. I can't risk getting tangled up in it."

"What are you saying?"

"Do the police have the murder weapon? Guns are easily traced."

"Get out of my house," she said through her teeth. Her fingernails cut into her palms.

"Dana—"

"Get out!"

"Now you're being unreasonable. You can't be selfish about this. You have to think about how your actions reflect on others. You have to think about the consequences."

"Unreasonable. No, *dear,* this is unreasonable." She reached across the counter and jammed the dirty sponge into his coffee cup. "Now, get out of my house."

With cool dignity, he pushed the cup away. "I have no choice except to report the loss of the gun to the police. It upsets me as much as it upsets you, but I have to look out for my best interests."

"This is . . . this is the absolutely lowest, most despicable—you'll do anything to get even with me, won't you? I dared to tell Mr. Perfect no and now you get your revenge."

He stood, his shoulders back and his chin high. "Our former relationship has nothing to do with anything. I have certain responsibilities."

"Get out." The mop tempted her. Swinging the mop, chasing him off her property, getting in a few whacks against his perfectly moussed and blow-dried hair, held such immense appeal it frightened her. Instead, she turned her back on him. "I mean it, Neal, get out before I do something really stupid."

"I'm leaving." The stool legs scraped the floor. "I just hope," he said, slowly and with emphasis, "if someone were foolish enough to steal a firearm and that someone was also foolish enough to shoot a man with it, that someone would also have the sense to dispose of the weapon most carefully. Throw it in a river, perhaps. Or bury it out on the plains." His shoes clicked on the linoleum and he was gone.

The front door slammed.

Shaking began in her midsection and shivered outward, gripping her knees and arms and shoulders. Tears fell hot and fast. Her entire world was crumbling, disintegrating from under her feet, and for the life of her, she couldn't see a single way to stop it.

Chapter Six

Kurt hopped up onto the small covered porch before Dana's front door. He rubbed his sweaty hand across his thigh before he rang the bell. Spring in Texas meant crazy weather, and today was no exception. It had started out cold this morning with a brisk wind. By noon, the wind had died and hot humidity settled over the city. Storm clouds hovered, containing the heat like a lid on a simmering pot. His shirt clung to his back.

While waiting for Dana to answer, he admired the house. Small and tidy, it was a one-and-a-half-story French provincial with curved window heads and brick quoins on the corners. It sat at the top of the cul-de-sac, perched on a low hill that put it above its neighbors. The landscaping was lush and green, rimmed with beds of irises, tulips and hyacinths.

The door opened and Dana invited him to enter.

"Did you make that list about Tuesday?" he asked, looking over the airy foyer and curved staircase. She didn't have much furniture, but what she did have was good quality. He liked her taste, which was elegant but not fussy.

"Hello to you, too," she said. "Yes, I made a list."

Her scratchy voice alarmed him. As his eyes adjusted to the indoor light, he could see her swollen eyes. If her feverish complexion was any indication, she'd indulged in a world-class crying jag.

"Everything okay?" he asked.

"Peachy." Slump-shouldered, she walked through the narrow dining room and into the kitchen.

Kurt followed. The place looked as pristine as a model home and smelled strongly of cleansers. A picture formed in his mind of her scrubbing and weeping. It hurt his heart.

He tossed the sack he carried onto the kitchen counter.

"The only unusual thing that happened on Tuesday was I went home early." She showed him the sheets of paper she'd covered with lists of everything from what she'd eaten on Tuesday to everyone she'd spoken to on the telephone and talked to in person. "I had Jilly, my secretary, confirm calls and appointments. This is as accurate as I can make it."

Nearly head-to-head with him, she went down the list. Her slender finger with its perfect oval nail distracted him. She had the prettiest hands he'd ever seen, slim and smooth-skinned. Her scent distracted him, too. Underneath the smell of household cleansers lingered sweet womanliness.

She shuddered and turned away, and her narrow back rose and fell with a heavy breath.

"Dana?"

She shook her head. "Would you like something to drink?" Her voice was high-pitched and shaky.

"It's okay," he said. "There's nothing wrong with crying. Other than the obvious, did something happen to upset you?"

She sagged against the counter and covered her face with a hand. "I'm all right. I just...it hit me today how much trouble I'm in."

He sensed a lie. Or at least, evasiveness. The newspaper lay folded on the countertop. Other than the photograph, the story had barely mentioned her. He didn't think it would reduce her to tears. "Talk to me. That's what I'm here for."

She pulled large glasses from a cabinet and filled them with ice. "You do think I'm innocent, don't you?"

"Sure. So who doesn't? Did the cops come by?"

She filled the glasses with iced tea. "Sugar? Lemon?"

"Talk to me. That's an order."

"I am not in the mood to take orders from you."

"Yeah, like you'll ever be in the mood. Do it, anyway."

A weak smile curved her lips. "You're impossible."

He caught her hand as she passed and tugged gently. Her skin was hot. "Tell me what happened."

Halting and hesitant, she told him about Neal Harlow. A single tear leaked from her eye and she dashed it away with an impatient swipe. "I have made such a mess of my life."

He urged her to sit on a stool so she faced him. "What do you mean?"

She traced idle patterns on her knees. "I work seventy, eighty hours a week. I haven't had a real vacation since college. I always thought I had lots of friends, but... they're business relationships. Shallow. I haven't had time to be a good friend to anybody, and now I realize..."

"You feel alone. Deserted."

She nodded and swiped at her eyes again. "It's my own fault. My life is so compartmentalized. Everything I do is by appointment only. Up until yesterday I thought my life was perfect. I thought I had it all. Nice house, nice car, good business, but that's all window dressing. The only thing keeping me from falling apart completely is knowing my parents will be home next week."

"You've got me."

She laughed weakly. "I barely know you."

He placed two fingers under her chin and lifted her face. Though raw from tears, her eyes were still beautiful. The vulnerability in them touched him deep inside. "Hey, I'm your white knight and you're my fantasy blonde. How can we go wrong?"

She laughed again.

He patted her cheek. What he wanted to do was hold her and kiss her and show her he'd never let her down. He forced himself to turn away. "So to hell with Neal. We've got work to do. Why did you go home early on Tuesday?"

Her faint smile returned. "To hell with him? That's all you have to say? He's going to tell the police I stole his gun."

"I can beat him up for you." He ground a fist against his palm.

Her blue eyes sparkled. "Don't tempt me."

"Forget him, then. We've got more important things to worry about."

"Worry?" She gazed with trepidation at the paper sack he'd brought. "More worries, you mean?"

"Kind of, sort of. I heard Callister and Tannenbaum found something when they searched your office. I don't know what it is, but it's got them excited."

She stiffened. "They couldn't possibly find anything."

"I just hope none of your employees stashed any drugs at the office. I've got people checking into it. Right now, let's talk about Eddie Gordon. You're absolutely positive you've never seen him. Not even just in passing. Seen him hanging around."

"I'm absolutely certain I didn't recognize him."

"So let's go back to Tuesday. Why did you leave early?"

She looked at him askance. "It was a slow day and I was tired. And I didn't go home that early. I usually stay at the office until seven or eight, but I left around five-thirty on Tuesday."

He picked up her list. "All these people you talked to, they can confirm it?"

"I suppose so. Is it important?"

"We need an alibi, Dana. So how about the woman who wanted to meet you at O'Dooley's. Do you remember anything else about her?"

She caressed her sweating glass, then smoothed her damp hand down the length of her throat. The sight arrested Kurt. Soft light coming from outdoors highlighted the sculpting of her profile and the elegant curve of her throat. Surely he'd seen or known more beautiful women, but he couldn't recall a single one.

"She called on Monday. I can't remember the time or even if it was morning or afternoon. I asked Jilly, but she can't remember what time it was, either. The only thing both of us are certain about is she didn't give her name. That's why I didn't meet her. I'm not into mysteries." She glanced at him, did a double take and frowned. "Why are you looking at me like that?"

Something about her tugged at him in ways he hadn't been tugged in years. "I'm not. Go on. Why did you note it on your calendar?"

"Habit? People give me information, I write it down. Wait a minute, I do remember something. She had an accent. A thick country accent." As soon as she said it, she rolled her eyes.

Kurt guessed the reason for it. Dallas was an urbane city, but "country" accents were common as dirt. "So she gave no reason why she wanted to meet you at O'Dooley's."

A faint line appeared between her eyebrows. "I can't remember anything she said. What's in the sack?"

"A copy of the videotape."

She made a strangled little sound. "How did you get it?"

"I asked, they gave it up. Don't think it's out of the goodness of their hearts, though. Like Greeks, beware of cops bearing gifts. They must be hoping you'll look at it and decide to confess." He scowled at the papers. "What's this mean?" He stabbed a finger at a line she'd crossed out with a pencil slash.

She glanced at what she'd written. "Jilly reminded me about the office doors being unlocked. But that was on Wednesday, not Tuesday."

"Tell me about it."

"There's nothing to tell. Jilly is always the first to arrive, and she found my office unlocked. But it was probably the cleaning people, because nothing was taken and there was no sign of a burglary. Can we look at the tape now?"

"In a minute." No matter how he looked at her list, he didn't see how it offered an alibi. The murder had happened around nine-thirty at night. According to her list, no one could verify Dana's whereabouts after seven-thirty. Six witnesses, a videotape—they needed a miracle. "I went to O'Dooley's last night. It was the bartender who fingered you initially, and it's just like I figured it. He saw your picture in the paper and showed it around. Everyone agreed it was you. We may be able to show some kind of collusion. Have you got a copy of the newspaper story?"

She cast a longing look at the sack containing the videotape before she left the room. He watched her hips swaying under the soft fleece of her sweat suit. She was so beautiful it made him hurt.

She soon returned with a clipping.

It was standard schmaltz: Dana and Pauline pointing at a rack containing reels of computer disks. Dana stood with her head high and shoulders back, as poised as a fashion model. For a newspaper print, it was a surprisingly good likeness.

"What did the bartender tell you?"

"He says a woman came into the bar. He noticed her because—" he shot her a grin "—she was very attractive. She sat at the end of the bar near the door and ordered a ginger ale—"

"That proves it. I despise ginger ale."

Kurt made a note of it. "She didn't talk, but he says she appeared to be waiting for someone. He got busy, and the next time he noticed, she was walking out with Eddie Gordon."

"Not only do I not drink ginger ale, but I don't hang around in bars. I certainly don't allow strange men to pick me up." She crossed her arms on the countertop and shook her head in vehement denial. "Do you think I'm being set up?" Her voice faltered to a mumble. "Doesn't make any sense."

It didn't make sense to Kurt, either. He'd considered the possibility of somebody using a double to set up Dana and frame her for murder. The how seemed unlikely; the why seemed impossible.

Her fingernails clicked softly on the counter. "A woman calls me out of the blue and asks to meet at a bar where I've never been. She has to be the killer."

"I agree."

"But she looks just like me? That's not a coincidence, that's spooky. Besides, no one has a motive to do this to me."

He grunted in disgust.

She picked up on his reaction, and her hand turned white-knuckled on her iced-tea glass. "Does somebody have a motive?"

"I'm worried about your motive." Her instant outrage made him add quickly, "I told you already. It's the drug angle. We have to deal with it."

"I see," she said, dragging out the words.

"I'll arrange for a blood test. We'll run a full-scale toxicology and cut the cops off at the knees."

She crossed her arms and laid her head atop them. "I feel as if I've fallen through a rabbit hole and ended up in nightmare land. So now, not only am I a killer, but also a thief who steals guns *and* a drug addict."

"Yeah, well, we'll deal with it when we get more information." He poised his pen to write. "Right now, tell me who knew about your picture going into the business section."

She closed her eyes.

"Isn't this a job for the police?"

"Fact of life, babe, they already have you. The only thing they're looking for now is anything that strengthens their case."

Her fringe of golden lashes fluttered. She straightened and picked up her tea. After several sips, she said, "Pauline, of course."

"Tell me about her." He'd drawn his own conclusions about Dana's perky little partner. Secure in her little universe around which everything else revolved, Pauline Kidder had a bad case of "me-itis."

She drew her head aside. "I don't like your tone of voice."

"No pussy-footing, no playing light touch with your dainty sensibilities. Somebody tried to get you to go to O'Dooley's. Whether you like it or not, you're involved somehow. So tell me about your partner." He printed Pauline Kidder on a sheet of paper.

She gave him "the look." "We were college roommates, and we shared an apartment after we graduated. She's honest and hard-working."

"You own the business fifty-fifty."

"Yes. Pauline is the computer wizard. She handles the technical side. I handle sales and administration."

"Any kind of rivalry? Bad feelings? Fighting over a man?"

She pushed away from the counter. "She's my best friend." She stalked to the French doors and looked out at the redwood deck in the tiny backyard.

Grudgingly, he admired her loyalty—stupid and misplaced though it may be. His brief encounter with Pauline had told him if the roles were reversed, Pauline would hang Dana out to dry. "Who else knew about the newspaper story?"

"Employees. The newspaper people. My parents. The reporter did the story three or four weeks ago. I can check my calendar for the exact date. I've talked to people about it." She turned on him and arched a brow. "I suppose you want a list?"

He cocked a finger at her. "Next to eyeballing a lovely lady, lists are my favorite things." His comment earned him a narrow-eyed glare. "Now, give me the real scoop on Pauline."

"I'm six inches taller than her. Even if she wore a wig, nobody could possibly mistake her for me. It has to be the woman who called." She caught her face in both hands and rubbed her temples with her fingertips. "Why would she ask me to be there? What if I had shown up?"

Kurt mulled it over. "Could be, she counted on you not showing up. You said it's a habit to write things down. Whoever set you up could know you very well."

A shudder racked her entire body. "Somebody studied me?"

"Stranger things have happened. Is there anybody who would benefit by getting you out of the way?"

"No."

"Don't answer so fast."

"Your question doesn't deserve an answer, fast or otherwise. I don't have that kind of enemies. Can we look at the tape now?"

"What happens to the business if you're out of the way?"

Hands on her hips, eyes flashing, she faced him squarely. "If you are entertaining any nasty suspicions whatsoever about Pauline Kidder, then leave now."

He entertained them all right. He was throwing a full-scale party, in fact.

TUESDAY, TUESDAY—another mundane day in a fairly mundane life. A life that used to be perfect and serene, the hours filled with business deals balanced by gentle pursuits. A life Dana feared would never be the same again.

Yet Kurt insisted on picking apart Tuesday, then Monday, then the previous week. He poked, probed, questioned, demanded clarification and explanations and dug through her memory with ferretlike tenacity. He made lists of her friends and acquaintances and business contacts. He demanded to know their roles in her life.

Finally, she held up her hands in a plea. "Please! No more! You're beating a dead horse. I don't know anything. Nothing out of the ordinary has happened. Nobody has ever threatened me. I don't have enemies. I didn't kill that man. I've never been to O'Dooley's. That's all I can tell you. May we look at the videotape now?"

Kurt tapped his pen against the countertop. The rat-tat-tatting pinged at Dana's nerves.

"I'm not asking to be nosy."

"I know." She refilled their iced-tea glasses. "I am cooperating to the best of my ability. I'm sorry I don't have an alibi. I'm sorry I can't prove I wasn't at O'Dooley's. But I'm doing the best I can."

"You know about worst-case scenarios? I deal with them almost every day."

"I believe I am dealing with one at this moment."

"You're not dealing with it, you're denying it. You're trying to be civilized, trying to make this situation fit into your neat little life. You're hoping the cops suddenly smack their foreheads and say, 'Gosh, we made a mistake.' I'm here to tell you, it won't happen. One solid piece of hard evidence is all they need to make an arrest stick.''

''I understand the seriousness of this.''

''Then get serious. We've got two options. One, we can be passive. Except, the cops have six eyewitnesses willing to testify they saw you with Eddie Gordon minutes before he was killed. Seeing is believing, babe. You'll be wearing prison blues before you know what hit you.''

He pushed off the stool and stalked through the dining area and family room. He paused before a framed poster of a knight atop a caparisoned charger. The knight swept a lady with Rapunzel-like tresses into his arms, prepared to ride her away from danger.

''Life isn't a fairy tale.''

She closed her eyes. ''I know that.''

''Then you better think hard about option number two.''

''Which is?'' she asked warily.

''We fight. Stop scrubbing that counter and pay attention.''

She looked down at the sponge in her hand. She hadn't realized she held it. She tossed it into the sink.

He returned to the stool. Watching her, he drank deeply from his glass, then wiped his mouth with the back of his hand. ''Let me tell you something about myself. I've got six brothers and sisters. In my house, sitting around waiting for something meant going without. If I wanted something, I worked for it, scrambled and fought. So that's me. I'm a fighter. I won't accept option number one. If that's what you want, get another attorney.''

"I'm not some pampered little fluff ball."

"Prove it. Start showing some backbone and stop whining about how hard it is. I know it's hard, but putting up a fight always is."

"Nobody has ever talked to me like this before," she grumbled.

He grinned. "We all do what we're best at, babe." He picked up his pen and wrote rapidly across the paper. "Okay. We have to answer some questions." He threw her a sharp look. "And no crap about it being the cops' job. Number one, the identity of the woman who called you, why she called and what she has to do with this. Number two, we have to find out exactly how certain those eyewitnesses are."

She breathed deeply, seeking her inner reserves. He was right. Like it or not, she'd been thrust into this nightmare and it was not going to go away. She either defended herself or resigned herself to an arrest, trial and prison.

"Come here." He patted his knee.

"No." She crossed her arms, holding her elbows. "I don't want you yelling at me anymore. We need to look at the videotape. I want to see if it's as bad as you said it probably is. That's the first thing we have to do."

His eyes lost their icy intensity. The way he looked at her jumbled her thoughts. No one, to her knowledge, had ever looked at her quite this way. He wanted her, with neither embarrassment nor ambiguity. He gave her the most overtly enticing, sexual look she'd ever experienced. Worse, she couldn't make herself look away.

He asked, "Do you like Greek food?"

Kurt acting like a barbarian was obnoxious; acting ferocious, he was scary. But her awareness of him as an attractive man who made no pretense about finding her desirable...

Her hands fluttered at her throat. "I do not understand you at all."

"Greek food," he repeated slowly. "Calamari, tiropetes, moussaka. Do you like it?"

"What does Greek food have to do with anything?"

"Taking you to dinner."

A funny little thrill tingled through her. She recognized her own desire, understood the deep primeval chord of response and even acknowledged the urge to accept the invitation in his eyes.

What she couldn't reconcile was why Kurt Saxon? Her Mr. Right was smooth and debonair, soft-spoken and gracious—wasn't he?

She grabbed the sack containing the videotape. She hurried into the family room and turned on the television and VCR.

Carrying both glasses of tea, Kurt sauntered after her. "So, you dated Neal."

"Pardon me?"

"Hard to see you and Neal as a couple. He's an officious little prig."

A laugh escaped before she could stop it. She forced a frown.

"I can see why he was interested in you, but what did you see in him?"

"Are you insulting me?"

"No," he answered mildly. "Just trying to figure it out. You seem too genuine for Neal's taste."

Snappy retorts failed her. He'd stated exactly why she couldn't love Neal Harlow. For all of Neal's good qualities, none were wonderful enough to excuse his continual status-seeking and obsession with how things looked.

He plucked the remote control from her hand and took a seat on the couch. She slid the tape into the VCR slot.

"You didn't answer me. Do you like Greek food?"

Don't encourage him, she warned herself. Don't look at him. Cops and killers were her concern, not Kurt's smile or the fluttery way he made her feel.

"I know a place with calamari that'll knock your socks off. I'd like to take you there."

She picked up his iced-tea glass and set it on a coaster before she joined him on the couch. She scooted as far from him as possible and curled her legs under her. "A date?"

He grazed her with a silky gaze, leaving goose bumps in its wake. "Yeah."

Where was inadvertent laughter when she needed it? "May we watch the tape, please?"

"Tonight. Eight o'clock."

He was looking at her like *that* again, leaving her stumble-tongued and unbalanced. She tore her gaze away from his. She'd been fending away unwanted advances practically all her life. She knew how to handle men. She knew how to say no and mean it.

All she had to do was make herself want to.

"We've got a lot of ground to cover. May as well do it in pleasant surroundings." His drawl deepened to a smoky purr. "Soft music, candlelight, a little dancing. Take your mind off your problems."

Indignation eluded her. Instead, images filled her head of his seductive voice whispering in her ear as he moved her slowly around a dance floor. She shook the image away. "Play the tape, please."

"All right, all right," he said with a chuckle. "Business first."

She stared at the television, half fearing what she might see. "You mentioned a polygraph before. That's a lie detector, right? I'm more than willing to take one. When can we do it?"

"It's tricky," he said with a grimace. "I can set you up with a polygraph. You can pay for it. Trouble is, the cops will say, you get what you pay for. I've got a request in for them to test you with a department examiner."

"I see." She wondered what difference it made.

"Polygraph results aren't admissible in court. It's an investigative tool only. Everything depends on how strong they think their evidence is. So keep your fingers crossed." He aimed the remote at the television and started the tape.

After initial static, a parking lot came into view. It was nighttime, but the parking lot was illuminated by lights on poles and from a neon array on the bar front. The camera focused on a pair of women, both brunettes. One was short and buxom, wearing a fringed leather jacket and cowboy boots. The other woman was tall and heavy, and she wore a long sweater that nearly reached her knees. In front of a shiny red car, the women mugged for the camera.

Kurt explained, "They're waitresses in the bar. The woman operating the camera is also a waitress. She had a new camera, the short woman had a new car. A match made in heaven." A disgruntled groan rumbled up from his chest. "I can't believe the quality."

The parking lot lights adequately compensated for the dark night. The picture was sharp and detailed.

Laughing and giggling, the women playacted a car commercial, pointing out the features of the new car and extolling its good gas mileage and powerful engine.

"Wait a minute!" Kurt stopped the tape and rewound it. "Look over on the left-hand side of the screen. The door to the bar."

Dana watched intently as the tape resumed. A man and a woman walked out of the bar. The man had his arm wrapped around the woman's shoulders. The light and distance made their facial features indistinct. The only identifying feature was the woman's hair, which was as pale as Dana's. The two of them moved out of camera range.

Dana twisted a strand of hair around her fingers. The faintest hint of gold kept her hair from being white. Not many adults had hair as pale as hers.

Kurt backed up the tape again. The couple were on screen for only three or four seconds.

The two women continued their horseplay. Then the camera audio caught a faint popping sound. The camera jiggled. The women looked offscreen, talking about the noise, asking if it was a gunshot, with the woman holding the camera saying it sounded like a car backfire. The image skipped—the camera had stopped filming and started again. The camera focused on the blond woman as she ran from between two parked cars. She staggered against the hood of a car, stumbled and nearly fell. She caught herself, jerked up her head and stared directly into the camera. The camera owner tried to use the zoom lens feature but did it too fast and the picture blurred. When the picture did come into focus, the woman was gone.

Dana straightened slowly and lowered her feet to the floor. Her hands curled into fists. Her heart pounded against her ribs. Air in the room acquired a syrupy bitterness. This couldn't be happening. It wasn't real. It couldn't be....

Kurt backed up the tape. Finding the frame where the woman's face was on screen, he froze the image.

"Good heavens," she whispered, "that's me."

Chapter Seven

Disappointment deeper than anything he'd ever felt washed through Kurt and left his chest heavy. Not only was the quality of the image on the tape far, far better than he'd expected, but the woman on the screen left little doubt about her identity.

He'd been wrong before, but rarely about people and never concerning anyone he felt as strongly about as Dana. He no longer wondered why the police allowed him to have the tape. This was no mere ace in the hole, it was the entire deck. Callister and Tannenbaum must be laughing their heads off thinking about Dana seeing this for the first time.

It seemed impossible for Dana's face to be any paler than what it was, but when the blood drained away, she appeared almost translucent. Slowly, she rose, and just as slowly she crossed the family room. As she raised a hand to the screen, light static crackled.

"Wow," Kurt breathed. He crouched beside her and looked between her face and the face on the television.

He searched for differences. A degree off in the slight tilt of her eyes, perhaps, or a not quite perfect straight and sculpted nose. The woman wore her hair pulled back, and her face appeared thinner than Dana's. Her cheekbones were slightly more prominent and her chin was sharper.

Dana glanced at him and gave a great start that knocked her back on her heels. "Don't look at me like that. That is not me! It looks like me, and... it looks like me." She jumped to her feet and briskly rubbed her arms.

"I've dealt with a lot of mistaken identities, but never with a doppelgänger. Or a clone. You taken part in any government experiments lately?" He heard the forced cheerfulness in his tone and hated himself for it. He did believe her. She was an innocent woman... wasn't she?

He peered closely at the screen. The woman held something in her hand. The angle and shadows made it difficult to see details, but enough was there to know she carried a gun. He stopped the tape and killed the volume.

"Serious now, no joke." He tossed the remote control from hand to hand. "I was hoping to bust the tape as too muddy or indistinct. I can tell you right now, in all confidence, that isn't going to happen." Visions of the video making national news sickened him. And it would. What would a jury think? He knew exactly what a jury would think. "Have you ever been in therapy? A psychiatrist or psychologist?"

She fussed with the filmy curtains over the French doors. "No."

"Ever suffered from blackouts?"

"Fainting? No."

He gave her an out and she ignored the bait. Which reinforced his belief in her, but wasn't making his job any easier. "Not fainting, blackouts. Periods of time you can't remember."

She turned on him. "I am not crazy. I don't suffer from blackouts or a split personality or some kind of Jekyll-and-Hyde thing. That is not me on the tape. Did you look at those clothes? I'd never wear a baseball jacket and I don't even own a pair of jeans." She pressed both hands between her breasts. "I've never seen that woman before in my life!"

The absurdity of her statement caught both of them off guard. Kurt laughed. Her full mouth curled into a sheepish smile.

She murmured, "You know what I mean."

A small laugh bubbled from her throat. Shaking her head, she eyed the television as if it might come to life and attack her. "I was hoping it was a wig and makeup making her look like me. But... not anymore."

He grinned. "Every time I feel sure I've seen it all, something like this happens. But I think you're right about the clothes. If the cops found bloodstained clothing or a weapon, we'd know about it."

"They'll just say I threw them away."

He played the tape again. Twice he watched the part where the woman ran into view. Her blue jeans clung to her buttocks and long legs like a second skin. Even if Dana owned a pair of jeans, she sure wouldn't wear them that tight.

"Buck up, I've got a friend," he said. "He's a private eye, the best in the business when it comes to missing persons. I'm going to put him to work finding our mystery woman. We will find her. At least we know what she looks like."

That last bit earned him a dry look before she wandered into the kitchen and opened the refrigerator. With one hand holding the door, she stared at the scanty contents.

"A private eye? We still haven't settled your fee," she said. She closed the fridge. "It's only fair to warn you that I haven't much ready cash. I had to borrow from my parents to raise the down payment on this house. Everything else is plowed back into the business. My credit is good, but I'm... overextended."

"You won't be the first to stiff me," he said absently. He considered ways to lessen the damage caused by the videotape. Other than physically producing the other woman, he didn't see anything. "Half my clients want to pay me in chickens."

"I have never *stiffed* anybody in my life. I pay my bills. All I am saying is it will take me a while to raise the money. You will be paid. Somehow. But if you need a retainer, I—I don't know what to do."

He frowned, thinking. Nobody had witnessed the actual shooting. The gun the woman carried was too indistinct for identification.

Which meant despite the tape, without a weapon or a confession, the police case was entirely circumstantial. "Don't worry about me. I'll cover the P.I.'s expenses and bill you later." He looked past her to the refrigerator. "Go change. We'll go to dinner."

"May I ask a favor?"

"Yes, you may," he said, unable to resist mocking her cool formality.

"Will you take me downtown to get my car, please? I feel trapped without it." She darted a look at the television and shivered. "I feel trapped in this house."

"No problem. Then we'll go to dinner."

"I'm exhausted."

"Buck up, Dana. The tape is worse than I hoped, but better than I feared. We'll beat it. You like Chinese?"

"Yes, but—"

"We'll get take-out and bring it back here. Chicken, beef, pork or seafood?"

"I didn't—"

"Ah, hell with it, I'll get some of everything. I'm starving." He flipped open the phone book and began searching for a nearby restaurant.

Dana gave up and headed for her bedroom to change. Kurt Saxon was impossible. He didn't listen, he treated her like some kind of army recruit who had better jump when he said jump, and he talked too fast. Always saying irrelevant things that were far too personal.

Grumbling made her feel better as she changed into a pair of slacks and a cotton sweater. She applied mascara to her lashes and a dusting of blush to her cheeks. Noticing her face in the mirror, she froze, seeing the other woman's face—or was it another woman? Was it possible she did suffer blackouts? She would know if she did, wouldn't she?

Such thoughts gave her the willies. She slid her arms into a linen blazer.

Kurt waited for her in the foyer. He leafed through a copy of *Antiques & Collectibles*. "You like old junk, huh?" he said, and tossed the magazine back on the hall table. "Fairy-tale books, dolls. Cute."

"It's no worse than collecting beer cans or junky old cars. It's certainly cleaner. Don't you have hobbies?"

"Sure. Playing softball, skiing, fishing."

"Harassing women," she said archly.

"That, too." He reached for the door handle, then stopped and gave her a crooked grin. "Sure you don't want to do the Greek place? A little wine, a little music. Do you some good."

"No, thank you. I am not in the mood for entertainment."

His smile softened.

She inhaled sharply. She worked well with people, she was good at sales and public relations. It should be the easiest thing in the world to establish a neutral working relationship with Kurt Saxon.

Should be . . . if his silvery gray eyes weren't so fascinating, and if he weren't so physically imposing, and if he'd stop surprising her with small kindnesses when she needed them the most.

"I've got this theory," he said. "There's no such thing as right time or right place. Stuff happens when it happens. Usually for no good reason. So you have to grab it when opportunity hits."

"Is that supposed to mean something?" Fighting her awareness of his attractiveness made her entire body ache. She didn't want to notice how his height perfectly complemented hers, or how his blue jeans fit with intriguing snugness.

"Neal calls and I'm in the middle of a softball game, my team is winning. I almost didn't answer the pager. But I did."

"What are you saying? This is fate?"

"Can you think of any other way I would have met you?" He glided a step closer. "We don't run with the same crowd." He fingered her jacket lapel. "We don't shop at the same stores."

She watched his hand moving slowly against her lapel. Heat spread through her belly. One more second and she'd end up rolling around with him on the floor.

"May we please go, *Mr.* Saxon? I'd like my car."

DURING THE DRIVE DOWNTOWN, Dana replayed the videotape in her head. The more she thought about it, the spookier it seemed. Folk wisdom said everyone had a double, but this was ridiculous.

She began wondering what *really* happened on Tuesday.

As she handed Kurt the credit-card-size electronic key to open the parking garage, she asked, "Do you think the private eye can find that woman?"

"If Austin can't find her, she doesn't exist." He slid the key into the slot. The indicator light turned from red to green, and a motor churned as the gate slid into the wall. He drove slowly into the garage.

Doesn't exist . . . Did Kurt believe she existed? "If we don't find her, I don't stand a chance."

He shook a finger at her. "Pessimism will give you wrinkles. Where's your car?"

"Upper level. Slot 134. What have I to be optimistic about? She looks exactly like me. I don't think my mother could tell the difference between us. Maybe Detective Callister was right about an evil twin."

Be honest, Dana. Was it you?

How could she know for absolutely certain there wasn't some deep, dark madness lurking in her subconscious? Some twist in her personality living a separate, secret life?

"The tape is damning. A jury would eat it up, but if it was enough, they'd make the arrest stick. They need hard evidence, like the murder weapon."

Disgust made her scowl. "Neal will make it easy for them." The attorney was history, she decided. Plenty of law firms in the Dallas area would be overjoyed to represent Star Systems.

"Purely circumstantial. That's if the gun he lost matches the murder weapon."

His matter-of-fact belief filled her with such gratitude, tears rose again. She squeezed her eyelids shut.

He stopped the Lincoln behind her blue Taurus.

She nodded and fished in her purse for her keys. "You'll have to let me go first. I have to use the key to get out."

He rested a hand on her forearm, and she stilled, staring out the windshield at the gloomy deserted garage.

"You still believe me," she said softly. "I mean, not just on technicalities, but you honestly know I'm not a killer." She held her breath, waiting.

"In all honesty, the majority of my clients shouldn't be walking the streets. My job isn't necessarily keeping them out of jail but in seeing they get fair treatment. It's a cruddy job, but I like the challenge."

The tape *had* changed his mind. He *did* think her guilty. Despair filled her, so heavy she doubted if she could rise off the seat. She wished her parents were home. She wished she were a child again, nurtured and protected. She wished—

"This is different. You're innocent."

She whipped her head around, staring at him in surprise.

"I keep throwing all I have at you, giving you outs, giving you chances to make excuses or explain things." He squeezed her fingers. "But, lady, you're clueless. So do me a favor and don't confess. You'll kill my faith in my instincts."

She mulled over his words. "In other words, you think I'm too stupid to have killed anybody."

His laughter filled the car. He gave her shoulder a playful push. "Love a gal with a sense of humor."

"Your sense of humor is very strange." She opened the car door.

He picked up her left hand. Always watching her eyes, he raised her hand to his mouth and kissed it, gently, warmly, a sultry brush of his lips against her skin that stole her breath away. Silvery glints shone in his eyes.

"I'll pick up the chow and meet you at your place." His exhalation tickled her wrist.

She stumbled from the car and stood in the humid, gasoline-scented garage, trying to catch her breath. She rubbed the back of her hand. The contrast between his roughneck appearance and the gallantry of the kiss made it all the more powerful. Her skin tingled. After giving herself a little shake, she slid determinedly into her car.

In the rearview mirror, she watched the black Lincoln and imagined Kurt behind the wheel, grinning and thinking he was hot stuff. Fine, the man knew how to make a grand gesture. Big deal.

Convincing herself it wasn't a big deal occupied her thoughts all the way home.

She guided her Taurus into the garage. As much as she hated to admit it, she was glad Kurt would soon arrive with dinner. Hunger had made her light-headed, but the very idea of actually having to prepare a meal exhausted her.

She didn't want to be alone, either.

She laughed at herself, admitting the truth. She liked the man, and disconcerting as he was, she enjoyed his company. He was single, she was single. A little flirtation never hurt anybody.

She grabbed her purse and stepped out of the car.

She caught a movement out of the corner of her eye. A hand grabbed her arm. A black-clad arm snaked across her chest and snatched her purse. Her attacker threw the purse across the garage, where it struck the wall and fell to the floor with a clatter.

Dana screamed. A hand slammed against her mouth, cutting her off in midscreech. Her knees buckled. She twisted and squirmed, kicking wildly and grabbing at his arm with her free hand. The assailant jerked her backward. She struck a solid body. The hand on her face squeezed with brutal force, threatening to dislocate her jaw. White-hot agony shot through her from wrist to shoulder as he wrenched her left arm.

"Hold still," a rough voice rasped against her ear. "Do what I say and nobody gets hurt."

Panic iced her muscles.

"Gordon was my buddy," he whispered. His breath burned along her cheek and the smell of onions made her gorge rise. "I ought to break your skinny neck. He was worth twenty of you." He shook her violently. "You and that squirrelly buddy of yours are like greased snakes, but your luck done run out."

He jerked her arm higher, driving her hand between her shoulder blades. Every muscle in her back and shoulder screamed. He urged her toward the door.

Her breathing rushed in her ears like waves pounding against a shore. Her heart thumped raggedly against her ribs and she felt certain he was ripping her left arm from the socket, but her head cleared, time seemed to slow, and each step was like wading through molasses.

She could feel his face against her hair. The hand squeezing her wrist had fingers of iron. Did he have a weapon? A gun or a knife? Why twist her arm if he did?

"Nobody gets hurt if you do exactly as I say. Open the door."

She didn't believe him for a second. At the first chance he got, this horrible man was going to hurt her badly. Through the thin sole of her shoe she felt the step. "The door is locked," she said against his hand.

He eased the pressure on her face.

"The door is locked," she repeated. "I dropped my keys. I can't open it."

He made a disgruntled sound. His movements against her back told her he was looking around. For the keys? For witnesses? She had to keep him out of the house. If he gained entry, she would die. She searched frantically for a weapon.

He shifted suddenly and the pressure of his body left her back while his grip tightened on her left arm. He kicked the door.

Wood cracked and metal popped, but the door held. He drew back, ready to kick it again.

The automatic garage door light went out.

Her assailant stumbled. Dana braced her feet against the step and shoved, using all the power in her legs to drive the man against the wall. He cried out hoarsely. A heavy thud was followed by a crash as a shelf collapsed, dumping its load of paint cans and cleaning supplies. Glass shattered. Cans clanked.

Dana scrambled to her feet and ran.

He caught her just as she reached the garage door opening. He spun her in a circle and knocked her to the ground. She hit the concrete with stunning force. Dazed, she felt him flip her onto her back. He straddled her belly, crushing her, pinning her hands to the icy floor.

"Stupid! You stupid little . . . the game is over! You lose," her assailant growled. "I want those pictures."

Spots danced before her eyes. It took several breaths before she could speak. "Pictures? I—I don't know—"

He squeezed her wrists cruelly. Tears burned her eyes.

"I know you got 'em. Your buddy turned on you, ratted you out. So don't play stupid with me! Where are they? You got the Dragon-man on you now. It ain't worth holding out, Dana."

Hearing him use her name frightened her more than the physical violence. She couldn't see him, didn't recognize his voice, but he knew her. "I don't know what you're talking about."

"You better figure it out real fast. Did he get to you? Warn you? I don't know what your game is, but I know you lose 'cause—"

Dana recognized the rattling rumble of the powerful engine. Kurt! With renewed vigor, she bucked and fought with all her strength.

Her attacker muttered an oath and jerked upright, dragging her up with him.

"Freeze!" Kurt bellowed.

Dana tried to scream, but Dragon-man wrapped his arm around her throat, choking off her breath. She clawed at his arm, but he held her fast. Her lungs contracted in an agonizing spasm.

"Turn her loose!" Kurt yelled. "Back off!"

Against her ear, her attacker whispered, "I'll be back. You even think about turning the pictures over to the cops and I'll take you apart a chunk at a time. The world ain't big enough to hide."

He shoved her. She stumbled, flailed her arms, frantically sought her footing.

Strong arms caught her. The sound of pounding feet receded and then were gone.

Dana's muscles relaxed and she slumped. Kurt prevented her from sliding to the ground. I'm alive, she thought, he's gone and I'm alive. . . .

Kurt scooped her into his arms and carried her to the door. He hit the garage door closer; the big door rumbled down. He shouldered his way into the house.

Dana began to laugh. Dragon-man had believed her about the door being locked. He hadn't even tried the knob. She'd lied to him and saved her life.

"Okay, babe, come on, it's okay, don't get hysterical on me." He turned on a light.

"I'm not hysterical. Put me down." She hiccoughed, choking down the laughter. She was safe, everything was okay. The bad guy had taken one look at Kurt and fled. Not only stupid, he was a coward, and he was gone.

Kurt's brow crinkled with worry, and his eyes anxiously searched her face. He ran his hands up and down her arms and over her back. His touch felt good, he made her feel safe and protected, and she wanted nothing more than for him to hold her forever.

"I'm all right," she said. "He didn't hurt me, not really." She caught his face in both hands. "You really are my white knight."

She kissed him.

Chapter Eight

Kissing Kurt Saxon was akin to eating chocolate: once started, it was difficult to stop.

His lips were firm and supple, both giving and demanding. In response to her hands sliding around his neck and to the pressure of her body, his posture shifted from protective to possessive.

The feel of him drove away the fear, and any urge to laugh.

She pulled away. He nibbled her lower lip, pressed hot, soulful kisses over her cheek. She pushed his shoulders. "Oh," she said breathlessly.

With open reluctance and a disgruntled sound, he loosened his grip, bringing his hands to her shoulders as if fearing she might fall. His eyes were dark and hot behind heavy lids. He guided her to the couch. Crouched at her feet, he examined her arms where Dragon-man had left finger-shaped welts on her wrists. "You're sure you're okay."

"Please stop looking so worried." His anxious concern arrowed straight to her heart. He cared, he genuinely cared. "I'm not hurt. He just scared me."

Groaning, Kurt dropped his head onto her lap. "Scared me, too," he muttered.

She combed his hair with her fingers and melted inside. If she wasn't very careful, she'd end up falling in love with this man.

"PICTURES," KURT SAID. He paced through the family room, pausing at windows and doors, searching the night for possible intruders. Impotent anger rattled him, knotted his belly. One police officer had responded to their call. One! He'd taken the report, looked over the garage, peered at Dana's bruises and promised he'd flag his report for Callister and Tannenbaum.

Kurt sensed the officer hadn't been overly impressed by their inability to describe Dragon-man.

"You're sure he said pictures."

"I told you exactly what he said," she replied testily. "Fifty times. He wants pictures, and he'll kill me if he doesn't get them."

Kurt picked up a carton of moo goo gai pan and dug into it, chewing automatically, without tasting. "All right, let's go over it again. The first thing he did was throw your purse away."

She glanced at the small leather handbag, now scarred from being thrown against the wall. "Yes."

"He threw your purse. He used your name. He knows you. I get it now."

"Please, no riddles. What do you get?"

"Your double gets nabbed at O'Dooley's. Only surprise, surprise, the lady was packing heat. So the first thing this goof does is toss your purse out of reach. He thinks you're armed. Dragon-man thinks your double is you."

She regarded him gravely. "The police think I'm a killer, and now killers think I'm a killer. Is that supposed to make me feel better?"

"It's starting to make sense. You said your office was open on Wednesday."

She sipped tea. "The cleaning people—"

"Think, Dana. You went home early, but that's unusual for you. So Gordon goes to your office after hours, thinking to find you alone. You aren't there. He breaks into your office, looks around for the pictures, can't find them. He notices your desk calendar. You have a date at O'Dooley's."

"Where he finds my double." She set down her tea and searched through the cartons of Chinese food. "Do you think she has the pictures? Is she impersonating me?"

"I doubt it. She took too much of a risk by contacting you. I think she was in the wrong place at the wrong time."

She nibbled fried rice. "How can we expect the police to believe all this when I don't believe it myself? I saw the way the policeman was looking at us." She held up her left hand and examined the redness. "I bet he thinks you did this to me. Did you hear him ask me if you and I fought a lot?"

"Did you tell him yes?"

"Stop making jokes."

Joke . . . that's how Callister and Tannenbaum were going to treat this. He could almost hear them: "Dragon-man, who nobody can identify or describe, wants pictures, and that's why a woman who could be Dana's identical twin killed Eddie Gordon. We'll get right on it. Thanks for the clue, man.''

"So let's find the pictures.''

She plopped the carton down. A few grains of rice flew onto the coffee table. She immediately wiped them up with a napkin. "What pictures? This whole thing is totally absurd. I haven't even touched my camera in months. The only person who's given me pictures lately has been my mother, and those are postcards from Hawaii.''

"Could it have to do with Star Systems? You handle sensitive material.''

"I don't handle it personally. Besides, it's all computer data, not pictures.''

"What about digital pictures? Computer images. Maps or something. Who handles the data?''

"Technicians. They accept data either on disk, or over the telephone through modems. Then they encrypt the data and store it on tape.''

"Encrypt?''

"The clients are provided their own passwords, sort of like a personal identification number for an automatic teller machine. If they need something, they can either come in and have the information put back on disks or they access it directly via modem, using their passwords.''

"Let's say I want to steal some data.''

"Even if you broke into the storage facility and took the tapes, they wouldn't do you any good without the passwords. If one of our employees transferred data onto a disk, it still wouldn't do you any good. Security is one of our guarantees. We store a lot of sensitive research data, along with things like customer lists and demographic information. Besides, anyone who knows our operation, knows that I don't have access. At least, not in a usable form."

"What about access to the passwords?"

"None whatsoever. Pauline is the only person who knows all the passwords."

"What if something happens to her?"

"If clients should happen to lose or forget their passwords, then a system is in place that calls for a lot of signatures and identification."

Kurt reasoned Pauline would make a better target if thieves were after information in Star Systems data banks. "All right. What about the buddy he talked about?"

"No name." She picked up an egg roll and eyed it glumly. "He said my buddy told on me. Ratted on me. I dare you to make sense out of that."

He finished the moo goo gai pan and selected an egg roll. Dana urged a napkin on him. He considered it dumb to worry about a few crumbs when he had more important things on his mind, but he used the napkin. After he finished the egg roll, he frowned at her. "Think about this. Has anyone given you a package lately, maybe on the sly? Maybe asked you to hold on to it until—"

Her eyes widened and she bolted upright. The remains of her egg roll fell from her fingers and bounced off the couch onto the floor.

"Dana?"

Her mouth opened and closed. She looked up at him with shocked eyes. "Carl," she whispered. Then stronger, "Carl Perriman. I got a package in the mail at work. Carl sent it."

Excitement fluttered in his chest. Now they were getting somewhere. He picked up the fallen egg roll and placed it on the coffee table. "Did he send pictures?"

"I don't know. When I realized it was from him, I stuck it in my desk. Pauline was upset and I didn't want to upset her further, and then the police came. It might be pictures."

"Who is Carl?"

She lowered her face. She picked crumbs off the floor. "He used to be our bookkeeper. And . . . he was a friend." She put her shoulder to him and shuddered with a painful-sounding sigh. "I had to fire him."

"What happened?"

"He embezzled funds from the company. About four thousand dollars. Carl had forged Pauline's signature on some checks. He swore he didn't do it, but there was no other explanation. I want to cry every time I think about it. It was just awful."

"Can you think of any reason why he'd send you pictures?"

"Other than photography is his hobby, not a single one." Dana slowly extended her hands, turning them back and forth as she examined the red marks and bruises in the light. "Carl's a bookkeeper, not a gangster. He made a terrible mistake when he stole from me, but he never could explain what happened or where the money went. I didn't want to fire him, I wanted to work it out, but I couldn't trust him. I had no choice in the matter."

"Does he have a drug habit? Addicts steal. Addicts get involved with goofs like Eddie Gordon."

Her troubled gaze wandered the room. "I don't know," she whispered. "I just do not know."

"We'll get the package tomorrow and find out."

THE NIGHTMARE JERKED Dana to sweating, shaking, gasping wakefulness. Bolt upright in bed, she flailed at the hands choking her throat. She gurgled, fighting away the fingers squeezing tighter and tighter. Her eyelids flew open.

Gradually the real world cut through the fog. The smell of perfume and hair spray, potpourri and lemon oil filtered into her consciousness. Crickets and the sleepy noises of her house, faints sighs and the far-away hum from the refrigerator, replaced her harsh dream-breathing. Her heart slowed.

But the fear lingered.

Unable to bear the questions swirling through her brain, she left the bed.

Cool air caressed her bare legs and arms. She found her robe. Maybe there was a movie to watch. Something mindless and silly, absorbing enough to make her stop thinking about Dragon-man and Carl and a mysterious doppelgänger who carried a gun.

Mindful of Kurt sleeping in the spare bedroom, she eased open her bedroom door and slipped into the hallway.

A light came on and at the same time, Kurt spoke her name. Her heart leapt into her throat and she caught the wall.

Bathed in light from the spare bedroom, Kurt stood in the doorway.

He wore only blue jeans, riding low on his hips. She absorbed the vision of his deep, broad chest, tapered waist and the way bands of muscle roped across his flat belly. Thick curls of black hair flared across his pectorals, reaching for the heavy ridge of his collarbone. His skin was the color of burnished oak.

When he was fully dressed, she could dismiss him as too big and sloppy, even awkward. Half-naked, he displayed graceful power, a fascinating assemblage of planes and angles, suppleness and strength.

Muscles she hadn't been aware of in a long time tightened deep inside her.

"Are you all right? What's the matter?" Burled with sleepiness, his drawl was pronounced, his rumbling voice carrying like a cat's purr.

"I'm okay. I . . . I couldn't sleep."

"Bad dreams?"

She started to say no, but a yes slipped out on a sigh. Resting her back against the wall, she closed her eyes. "I'm scared he's coming back." She clutched her robe closed at her throat. The silky fabric felt flimsy as tissue paper. "I'm so tired, but I can't sleep."

"It's probably the Chinese food. For such a skinny old girl who says she isn't hungry, you sure can pack in the chow."

She opened one eye. A smile captured her mouth. "You have a perverse way with words."

He agreed with a nod. "Want some company?" He crossed the hallway in two steps.

His scent struck her and her heart lurched. She smelled sleep on his skin and masculine heat. She could almost hear the snap inside as her senses awakened. Her bare feet luxuriated in the plush carpet and she felt the texture of the wall beneath the thin fabric of her robe. Her own breathing seemed loud and ragged.

"I always sleep with one eye open, Dana. You don't have to be afraid."

"I always thought I was a brave person. Willing to take risks." She laughed weakly. "But you were right when you said I've had a nice little life. Nothing bad has ever happened to me. I've never had to be afraid."

"Fear isn't always a bad thing. It keeps you on your toes. Besides, you handled that goof just fine. I'm proud of you."

She met his gaze. His eyes arrested her, stripped her of coherent thought. The expression she read in the dim golden light was dark with concern.

He reached toward her face. Her breath caught. Reason told her to move away. If he touched her, she was lost. Instinct and need held her still. His fingertips grazed the line of her jaw and smoothed across her cheek. Her eyelids fluttered. Need swelled inside her like a living thing, flexing and stretching, awakening with a sharp, aching hunger.

He lowered his mouth to hers. She stayed still, her back firm against the wall, confused by the desire he roused. His sweet-musky scent blossomed inside her head and his lips were cool. He worked his fingers through her hair, parting strands over her ear then behind it, touching and testing the curve of her skull and finding a tender place below her ear. Her nerve endings quivered, leaving her weak.

His teasing tongue asked a silent question, and she answered it with a tentative parting of her lips. He tasted like rain. She reveled in the intriguing contrasts of his strong teeth, slippery tongue, firm lips, and the intoxicating feel of his hand on her cheek.

Her breasts tingled and ached, her nipples swelling. Liquid heat filled her veins.

She turned her head aside. The taste of him lingered, potent as wine.

He raised his head, but remained where he was with his hand cupping the side of her face.

"We shouldn't do this," she whispered.

"Why?"

A thousand reasons came to mind. She didn't know him. He was all wrong for her. He wasn't her type. The timing was wrong. She wasn't the kind of woman who had casual affairs....

He felt too good.

She wanted him too much.

"Dana?"

She feared looking at him. Holding her breath, she willed him to leave her alone.

He turned away. "Get some sleep," he said gruffly. "See you in the morning."

She managed to sleep, but it was restless and uncomfortable, filled with disturbing, erotic dreams. When she finally pulled herself out of bed in the morning, she felt worse than she had the night before.

Knowing she'd have to face Kurt, she showered and washed her hair. She glumly regarded her face in the mirror. Puffiness marred the thin skin under her eyes and her mouth turned in an unhappy line. A bruise was tender to the touch on the underside of her chin.

Yet the Dragon-man's attack felt like a bad dream, upsetting and frightening, but not quite real. Memories of kissing Kurt was another matter altogether.

She'd dated many men. With all of them she'd been in control, setting her own terms, never allowing herself to be swept away or distracted from the course she'd set for her life. Kurt was different. Dangerous. A wild thing whose forceful personality was greater than his size. It might be possible to tame him, but he'd never be fully under control.

Even worse, around him she didn't feel in control. He knocked something loose inside her, something hungry and reckless. He set off her temper, goaded her into laughter, exasperated her, teased her—excited her.

Mostly he confused her.

She dried her hair, leaving it to fall straight and silky past her shoulders. A careful application of makeup disguised her fatigued eyes and the bruise on her chin. She dressed in her favorite sweater. Made of ice blue silk, it felt soft as rabbit fur, and the scooped neckline accentuated the swell of her bosom.

She suddenly laughed at herself. Dragon-man wanted to kill her, the police wanted to put her in prison—and she worried about looking nice for her outrageous attorney.

Halfway down the stairs, she smelled coffee. Kurt must be in the kitchen, waiting for her. She prayed he was fully dressed.

Something wicked in her half hoped he wasn't. He had his faults, but his muscular, beautifully toned, hundred percent male body wasn't one of them.

A man entered the foyer.

A strange man.

He looked up at her and smiled.

Chapter Nine

Air rushed from Dana's lungs and her heart squeezed as if a fist had grabbed it. *Run!* screamed the voice of panic in her mind. *There's nowhere to go!* screamed the equally panicky voice of reason. Clutching the banister with both hands, she stared at the man.

A black T-shirt outlined a torso showing not a trace of fat. Deadly power emanated from his compact body and there was a quietness about him, a sureness of energy surrounding him like an aura. He wore a holster on his hip, and the butt of a gun gleamed black in the sunlight through the windows. If ever a killing machine walked on two legs, this was he.

Dragon-man!

He looked at her with velvet dark eyes, unreadable as the surface of a mountain lake. "Want some coffee? I heard you in the shower, so I made a fresh pot." He headed for the kitchen.

Coffee? Her knees turned watery and she sank onto a step. Breathing hard through her mouth, she rubbed a fist over her heart, willing a semblance of a normal heartbeat. What kind of killer offered coffee?

When she was finally able to move, she crept to the kitchen. The man was reading the newspaper. A cup of coffee steamed on the breakfast counter. She slid onto a stool. If she was going to die, at least she could satisfy her curiosity first. She cleared her throat to catch his attention.

He gave her a small smile, the barest pull of his lips. "Austin Tack," he said mildly. "I'm a friend of Kurt's."

"Oh." The private eye Kurt had told her about.

"He had some business to take care of." He extended a hand over the counter. "Nice to meet you, Dana."

Dana hesitated, but good manners kicked in and she shook hands. His grasp was light, but firm, promising far more strength than he displayed. His eyes disturbed her. In contrast to his tawny hair, they were so dark they seemed black. Deep set, they were shadowed further by thick black lashes. "Kurt asked you to...watch me?"

He nodded.

As the adrenaline faded from her system, indignation grew. How dare Kurt presume to allow a stranger into her home. "How very kind of him. He might have said something."

"You were sleeping. Hungry?"

"No, thank you. Mr. Tack."

"Just Austin." He cocked his head, those black eyes seeming to absorb her. She focused on her coffee. Kurt's friends, apparently, were as strange as he was. "I've been studying the tape. I see it now." He picked up a coffee cup and headed for the family room.

Two things struck her at the same time. One, Austin's comment had been as certain as it was confusing, and two, the man didn't make a single noise. Not even a whisper of his shoes against the floor or the rustle of clothing. She followed him.

She settled on the couch and set her coffee cup atop a coaster. "What is it you see?" She couldn't believe she was having this conversation. For all she knew, Kurt was lying dead somewhere and this strange, quiet man was merely toying with her.

Austin regarded the remote control unit he held. "Catch," he said, and tossed it.

She flung up a hand reflexively and caught it.

"Yep." He sat on the chair closest to the television set. He tented his fingers over his chest and stared at the blank television screen.

Dana waited. She drank her coffee. She rubbed her wrist where the swelling had subsided, leaving finger-shaped bruises. Explanations, apparently, were not Austin Tack's style.

"Have you known Kurt long?"

"We were in the service together. Marines." He chuckled fondly. "After we got out, we ran a security service. We made pretty good money. That's how he paid for law school."

"He worked *and* attended law school?" Her own college days had been hectic and stressful. She couldn't imagine how she'd have graduated if she'd had to work, too.

"Yeah, and his wife hated it, but then again, she never did have a sense of humor."

A spasm clutched her diaphragm. "He's married?"

"Was." His dark eyes seemed to reach inside her. "He didn't tell you? They've been divorced five or six years. I don't know why he married her in the first place. All she cared about is stuff. Cars, clothes, fancy house, country clubs. Kurt never made enough money to satisfy her. She dumped him for an insurance broker."

Dana shifted uncomfortably. She sensed Austin was challenging her, or perhaps, warning her. Is that how he perceived her, a woman who cared only about stuff? His words reminded her of Kurt's contempt for Neal Harlow.

The garage door rumbled and a throaty engine announced the arrival of the black Lincoln. Austin rose, his right hand hovering casually over the gun strapped to his hip. He glided soundlessly toward the kitchen and paused, watching the short hallway leading to the garage.

Dana held her breath. If it wasn't Kurt who had arrived, would Austin shoot? If it was Kurt, would he shoot, anyway? Why was she sitting here like a dummy waiting to find out?

Kurt strode into the kitchen, slamming the door behind him. "Hey, man, is she up yet?"

Austin's shoulders relaxed. He nodded and returned to the family room.

From the couch, Dana watched Kurt sling grocery sacks onto the counter. He made several trips to the garage, ending up filling her kitchen with a collection of sacks and boxes. Dana considered asking him what it was, but if she did, he'd tell her and she'd be annoyed, because no doubt she didn't really want to know. As it was, she was annoyed, anyway, about Austin nearly scaring the pants off her.

Kurt strode into the family room. He smiled broadly at her, catching her off guard, again. His teeth were very white against his suntanned face.

She held her breath, wondering if he'd kiss her in greeting. Wanting him to do just that annoyed her most of all.

She pulled her features into her most forbidding expression. "I'd like to talk to you—" She noticed the cat.

It strolled behind Kurt, carrying its tail like a flag. A black-and-silver tabby, with long silky hair variegated in stripes, it was the largest cat Dana had ever seen. It hopped onto the back of the couch and regarded her through owlish eyes.

"What is this?" she whispered.

"Snooky." Kurt tossed a leather jacket on a chair. "If I leave him at the office, he gets bored and starts messing around with papers and stuff. He drives my secretary crazy."

"Snooky," she repeated stupidly. Something was going on here, but for the life of her, she couldn't imagine what.

"This works out great." Kurt raised his voice as he went to the kitchen to pour a cup of coffee. "I'm sick of sleeping at the office."

"What are you talking about?" She wanted to yell, but both the cat and Austin were watching the exchange with open interest.

"I told you about the fire in my apartment building and how I've been sacking out in my office. This will work great."

"What will work great?"

"My staying here." He waggled a hand back and forth. "But don't worry about me charging extra. We'll call it even."

She leapt to her feet. "Staying here?"

"You need a bodyguard."

She started to repeat what he said, but caught it, knowing she was beginning to sound like some sort of dim-witted echo. "You can't move into my house. I don't want anybody living in my house."

"It's no problem. You need a bodyguard, and there's no sense in your paying three or four hundred bucks a day to a stranger when I can handle it."

"Just what qualifies you as a bodyguard?"

Austin made an amused noise.

"Four years in the marines, a third-degree black belt and this." He patted the revolver holstered on his hip. "Austin will stand backup if necessary. Don't worry, you won't even know I'm here. Quiet as a mouse. And I'll cook."

She shifted her stunned gaze to the kitchen where Kurt's sacks and boxes covered the countertops. Not know he was here? That would be like trying to ignore a grizzly bear.

He grazed her chin with a knuckle. "Did you sleep good? You look better. I like that sweater." His gaze lingered for a moment on her breasts. "We have lots of work to do. You hungry? I got some groceries." Without awaiting her reply, he returned to the kitchen.

He was worse than impossible. He was infuriating.

Kurt and Austin put away groceries. The boxes, she noted, contained clothing, law books and files. He was not only moving in, he was taking over. Only the reminder about the Dragon-man in the form of deadly sidearms strapped to each man's hip kept her from complaining. She refilled her coffee cup.

Kurt tossed a package of hamburger to Austin who caught it easily. He examined the package and grunted in disapproval. Kurt laughed and made a disparaging comment about tofu and rabbit food. Dana found their camaraderie interesting.

"So, you looked at the tape?" Kurt asked.

Austin nodded.

"Can you find her?"

Austin nodded again. He began folding grocery sacks.

Kurt turned to Dana. "Austin is the P.I. I told you about. A two-legged bloodhound."

Somehow Austin didn't fit with her image of a private eye. She'd expected someone seedy, perhaps stinking of cigars. But then, why not? Kurt didn't look like an attorney, so why should his friend look like a private eye? "How are you going to find her? She could be anywhere."

"Leave it to me." Austin's mild, soft voice held firm conviction. "By the way, man, you missed it."

Kurt snorted. "I never miss anything."

"Did this time." Smiling enigmatically, he went to the family room.

As Dana slid off the stool, she whispered, "He's so quiet."

Kurt grinned and winked, giving her the idea there was a joke involved, but she hadn't a clue as to what it might be.

Dana and Kurt sat on the couch while Austin started the tape of the mystery woman. When he reached the part where the woman and Eddie Gordon emerged from the bar, he stopped the tape. He pointed to the woman's left hand. Though the shadows and lighting made the image indistinct, it was good enough to see the woman's hand inside her jacket pocket. Austin waited a moment before continuing. At the part where the camera caught the woman full front, he froze it again. He pointed to the gun.

"Left hand," he said.

His eyes fairly snapping with interest, Kurt leaned forward and stared intently at the screen.

Austin played with the forward and reverse control until he froze the tape at another frame. "Look at her jacket. The pockets have snaps or maybe Velcro fasteners. The left pocket is gaping, but the other is flat. I think our mystery woman is a southpaw."

Kurt whistled.

The corners of Austin's mouth tipped in a faint smile. "You, Dana, are right-handed."

Catching on, she nodded, her relief so great that she was unable to trust her voice. Now everybody had to realize it wasn't her on the tape. She wasn't crazy or afflicted with a split personality. She forgave Austin for her previous scare. She almost forgave Kurt for bullying his way into her home.

Austin fiddled with the tape again until he found the frame that showed the woman's face most clearly. "Check out the widow's peak."

Dana touched her forehead where her hairline dipped into a small peak.

Kurt looked between her and the television. Suddenly, he swept his hand over her brow, pulling her hair away from her face. "I'll be damned."

"What?" she cried and slapped his hand away. "What is it?"

"Mirror image," Kurt said. "Your peak is off center, it points to the right. But hers points to the left." He rose off the couch and crouched before the television. "Could the images be reversed?"

"This is video, not film. No negative involved," Austin replied. "What you see is what you get."

"THE POLICE HAVE TO believe it isn't me," Dana said.

Kurt stroked Snooky the cat, who arched his back and partially closed his eyes. After a moment, the cat jumped off Kurt's lap and hit the floor with a heavy thud. He sauntered into the kitchen.

Dana watched the cat explore. Like Kurt, Snooky seemed completely at ease in her house.

"It's open to interpretation. Just because she was carrying the gun in her left hand, doesn't mean absolutely for certain she is left-handed."

"The widow's peak—"

"It gives us something to work with, but we can't count on it. Don't worry. Austin will find her."

Austin Tack had left as silently as he'd appeared, armed with photographs of Dana.

"Our more immediate problem is figuring out the deal with those pictures. I talked to Tannenbaum this morning—"

"Why didn't you tell me?"

He raised a hand as if to fend her away. "Don't get your panties in a knot. I'm telling you now. He is not impressed with Dragon-man."

"He doesn't believe I was attacked."

"Look at it from their point of view. Callister and Tannenbaum carry a heavy caseload. Calling them overworked is a vast understatement. Some cases are more urgent than others. For instance, Callister is the primary in a cop-killing, and trying to solve it must be eating him alive." He showed the palms of his hands. "Then there's Eddie. A lowlife drug dealer nobody likes and nobody cares about. What the cops wanted was to have you say you shot him so they can go on to more important things."

"If they don't care, why can't they leave me alone?"

"It's their job. Besides, this case has political possibilities. I imagine they're getting pressure from the prosecutor's office. The last thing they need is us throwing in a mysterious goof called Dragon-man."

She sighed. "It does sound pretty stupid." She glanced at her poster of the knight. "Like something made up."

"Exactly. So let's go see if Carl did send you pictures."

"I still can't imagine Carl involved in anything illegal. He's very timid, shy."

"He stole from you for a reason. Could be he's supporting a habit."

"I just can't see Carl connected to drugs. Besides, it's pictures Dragon-man wants, not drugs or money." She opened her purse and made sure she had her office keys.

"Dana?"

Finding him right next to her gave her a small start. He stared intently at her, making her feel lopsided and warm.

"About last night."

The back of her neck prickled. "What about it?"

"It was nice."

Surprised, she looked up at him. She smiled. "I'll concede that." He was going to kiss her again. Enfold her in those big arms and hold her tight and make her feel real in an increasingly unreal world. His hands would do delicious things to her body and she'd touch again his solid chest.

"Good. Let's go."

Her mouth dropped open. She stared at his back. "Nice? That's all you have to say?"

. He glanced over his shoulder. "If you're looking for an apology, remember, you kissed me first. Let's go."

"I don't expect an apology. I . . ." What she expected eluded her completely. "Oh, never mind." She slung her purse over her shoulder and hurried after him.

She didn't speak to him until they reached the highway and he maneuvered his car into the fast-paced traffic. It took that long before she trusted herself not to sound like a frustrated, sex-starved harridan. "What happens if we do find pictures?"

"We'll figure out if they hurt or help."

"How could it hurt? I'm not involved in anything illegal."

He pulled a face. "Carl sent them to you for a reason."

She didn't want to know what kind of suspicions he harbored. Arms crossed, she glared at the clutter around her feet.

"Suppose Carl latched on to something hot. So he made copies and sent you a set for insurance. You're a trusting soul. A friend gives you something, you take it at face value. You don't ask questions. You don't snoop."

"You make me sound naive."

"Aren't you?"

"No!"

He laughed. "If I gave you a box and asked you to store it in your garage, would you look in the box?"

"Of course not."

"That's my point." He grinned cockily. "I'd look in the box."

"Just because I respect a person's privacy, doesn't make me naive."

"It does make you the perfect patsy."

"I resent that."

His smile widened, showing his teeth. He glanced at the rearview mirror, did a double take, and his smile disappeared. Under a glowering brow, his eyes glittered like shards of ice. "Damn it."

"What is it?"

"We've got a tail."

Her heart thudded against her ribs and she sank lower on the seat. "Dragon-man? Do you think he has a gun?"

"I recognize the car. I'm sure it's a reporter. Hold on." He accelerated, then cut sharply into the right lane. A Toyota honked frantically behind them.

Dana grabbed the dashboard with both hands and squeezed her eyes shut. The Lincoln rocked and groaned. The tires thump-thumped and the force of a turn pressed her against the door. She peeked. Kurt drove around a cloverleaf exit and headed for the ramp taking them back onto the highway.

"There he goes." He pointed down the highway. "The red Ford." He took his time merging back into traffic.

"Are you sure it's a reporter?" Being attacked by Dragon-man in the dark had nearly given her a heart attack. Meeting him face-to-face . . . She shuddered at the thought.

"That or a cop," Kurt replied. "Since Eddie Gordon probably doesn't merit the funds or manpower needed for a surveillance operation, my vote is for a reporter. You do realize, sooner or later, probably sooner, somebody is going to leak the videotape to the press."

Dana was horrified. Seeing the videotape had almost convinced her she was a killer. What would the public think? What would her parents think? Imagining how they would react was too distressing to think about. She prayed to have this mess straightened out before they returned from their vacation.

At the Baylor building, they rode the elevator upstairs to the seventh floor. The hallway was lit, but every door was closed and locked and all the offices were dark. Dana used her key to enter Star Systems. Lights were on in the reception area.

"Who works on the weekends?" Kurt asked.

"It's probably Pauline." Still stinging from their last encounter, she didn't have the heart to face her partner right now. She urged Kurt to follow her into her office. She closed the door softly behind him.

Everything looked normal. She pulled open the drawer where she'd placed the package from Carl. Hanging file folders crammed toward the back told her the drawer had been searched. It relieved her immensely to find the envelope where she'd left it. She handed it to Kurt.

He studied the envelope. Snorting softly, he pointed out the postmark. "You got it Thursday? It took ten days to get across town from Garland. Good old U.S. Mail." He shook the contents onto the desk. "Well, well, look here."

The envelope contained a supermarket film developing packet and a folded sheet of paper. Dana had been expecting photographs, but seeing them dismayed her, anyway. No doubt about it now, Carl was involved. First he embezzled, then he turned the Dragon-man loose on her. How had she so misjudged him? She'd trusted him, considered him her friend.

Kurt dealt the photographs like cards, spreading them across her desktop. He muttered, "Never seen anyone with such a clean desk. You sure you work here?" Then, softer, "I don't get it."

Puzzlement growing, she rested her hands on the desk and leaned over the photographs. She didn't get it, either.

All the pictures were of Pauline and Neal Harlow. The sky was overcast, melding into the background of cypress trees. They wore coats, and wind blew their hair.

Kurt pointed out a photo showing a bench. "Looks like they're in a park."

She picked up a photograph of Pauline and Neal embracing, locked in a passionate kiss. The pose was suitable for a perfume advertisement. Knifelike pains sliced across her abdomen.

Tossing the photograph back on the desk, she turned around. "So Neal and Pauline are having an affair. Big deal. She has affairs with everybody." She couldn't help wondering when Carl had taken the pictures. Or why he had sent them—unless he wanted to hurt her feelings. In that case, he'd accomplished his purpose in spades.

Kurt unfolded the sheet of paper. "It's a letter. 'Dear Dana,' it says. Want me to read it?"

"Go ahead."

Kurt cleared his throat.

"You were the best friend I ever had. So please believe me when I say I am not doing this to get even or just to hurt your feelings. Pauline Kidder framed me. She stole the money, not me. I don't have proof yet, but I am getting there. I have her under surveillance. These pictures prove she doesn't care if she hurts you. She doesn't care about anything but herself. Do not trust her. I will always be your friend. Love, Carl''

Kurt looked up. "That's it."

Dana slid onto her chair and rested her chin on her fist. Glumly, she eyed the array of photographs. Pauline and Neal walking hand in hand. Pauline and Neal facing each other, staring longingly into each other's eyes. Pauline and Neal kissing.

Even read in Kurt's deep-voiced drawl, Carl's pain and indignation came through loud and clear. Nausea made her head spin.

Kurt gathered the photographs into a stack and smacked them lightly on the desk. He slipped them back into the packet. "My question is, do you believe Carl? And if so, do you think Pauline would hire a goof like Dragon-man to keep you from seeing these pictures?"

"Now you're being absurd. Neal and I broke up. It doesn't matter if she's seeing him." Kurt's silence wore on her, made her itchy. "We're talking about people with guns. Even if Pauline is a man-stealing little liar, it doesn't mean she'd have anything to do with Dragon-man."

"So maybe she doesn't care if you know about Neal. What about the embezzlement? If she framed Carl in order to cover her tracks, how much further would she go?"

"She wouldn't hire Dragon-man."

"What about setting you up for murder? How much is this business worth?"

She didn't like where she sensed this was leading. "We grossed over six hundred thousand last year." She suddenly clapped her hands over her ears. "No! Pauline has her faults. I might even believe, with enough proof, that she stole from the company. But what you're thinking is grotesque."

"Yeah, what am I thinking?"

"That she arranged for an imposter to frame me."

"Fun to consider, but I don't see how it's possible. I'm thinking more along the lines that Pauline's antics go a lot deeper than we suspect. She's got a lot more to hide than playing kissy-face with your boyfriend."

"He's not my boyfriend!"

"Obviously not. He's going to tell the cops you stole his gun."

It took a few seconds for his implication to sink home. "Do you think they're conspiring against me?"

Frowning, he tucked the photographs and letter back into the mailing envelope. "If these are the photographs Dragon-man wants, then sure as hell something is going on. I'll accept a conspiracy."

"If Pauline wanted these pictures, she could have gotten them out of my desk."

"Maybe she didn't think you'd be dumb enough to leave them at work. She sure isn't going to ask you for them."

She opened her mouth to argue but remembered Pauline waiting for her in her bedroom. What had Pauline been doing while Dana showered? Searching the room, perhaps. Was that why she'd been at the house and so very curious about what the police might have found?

Distressed by suspicion, she hugged herself. She stared at the telephone. "We don't know these are the right pictures." Flipping through her Rolodex file, she found Carl's home phone number. She dialed and got a busy signal.

"Let's go see if we can find Carl." Kurt urged her off the chair. "Where does he live?"

"Over in Garland. Near Watson Park." She covered her eyes with a hand. "This is so depressing. After all this came out and I fired Carl, I cried for days. I hated myself. We were such good friends. He's a funny, shy little . . . nerd. I don't mean that in a derogatory way, not at all. He's just so innocent. My parents adored him, they practically adopted him. Daddy owns a boat, and he was always dragging Carl along on a fishing trip. My mother was just crushed when all this happened."

"You're crushed."

"Oh, Kurt, what if he's telling the truth? Did I do to him what the police are doing to me? I thought I had proof. My heart told me Carl wouldn't do such a thing, but I had evidence and I couldn't ignore it. And Pauline swore . . . oh, if she lied to me, I don't know what I'll do."

"It's been my experience that lying is second nature to most people."

"Not in my circle." She snatched her purse and headed for the door. She stopped short and spun on her heel. "Wait a minute!"

Kurt stopped in time to keep from bowling her over. "What is it?"

She slapped at the envelope he carried. "Those can't be the pictures Dragon-man wants. He said to me, if I go to the cops, he'll kill me. How could anyone possibly care if the police saw those pictures? You're the lawyer, is boyfriend-stealing a crime in Texas?"

"Boyfriend-stealing, good one, Dana." He chuckled, but seemed more bemused than amused. "Are you sure that's what he said?"

She shivered with the memory. "Something close to it. Yes, I'm sure."

Kurt scratched his head and pursed his lips. He studied the envelope front and back. "Good point. Have you received pictures from anyone else?"

"No." To make certain, she sorted through her in-basket, checking inside each envelope and folder. No pictures. She grumbled in frustration and headed for the door.

"Buck up, babe. We'll figure out what's going on." His smile rattled her to her toes. He arched an eyebrow. "Do you get tired of people telling you you're beautiful?"

She lifted her chin. "Please don't flirt with me."

"Why?"

"Because..." Coherent thought failed her.

"Because why?"

She cleared her throat and shifted her weight from foot to foot. "This is a ridiculous conversation," she said, far weaker than she wanted. "I appreciate all you're doing for me, but you and me, it would never work."

"Never say never." He lifted a strand of her hair and rubbed it between his thumb and forefinger. He gazed upon it as if it were a precious work of art.

Dana found it increasingly difficult to regulate her breathing. "These are difficult circumstances."

"I know. Weird, isn't it?" He swept her into his arms and kissed her.

A hard kiss, his lips and tongue forcefully demanding. A passionate kiss, blazing fiery trails of delightful sensation from her head to her toes. A sweet kiss, making the world disappear, consuming all her senses, making it impossible to believe anyone existed except Kurt Saxon.

When he released her, she staggered and caught the doorknob for support. His great chest heaved, once, twice. Moisture gleamed like dew on his lips. His eyes were black pools ringed by silver, compelling her to step over the edge.

"I feel it," he said, his drawl pronounced and husky. "You feel it. One of these days we'll have to do something about it."

She could almost hear her libido chuckling wickedly, mocking her indecision. She fumbled the door open.

Pauline said, "What are you doing here?"

Dana and Kurt stepped out of the office, Dana turned her back on her partner. She took her time locking the door and checking to make sure it was secure. More than anything in the world she wanted to confront Pauline with what she knew. She wanted to yell and to demand and force the woman to tell the truth.

But what was the truth?

She made herself turn around. "I had to pick up some things from my desk. What are you doing?"

Pauline darted a glance at her office. The door was ajar. "Uh, well, you know—"

"Pauline?" a man called from inside her office. "I think I found it. It's the morals clause. Strictly translated, it means one of the partners involved in drugs or alcoholism or embezzlement, but—" Neal stepped out of the office. He held a sheaf of papers. "Oh. Dana."

Dana looked from her partner to the attorney and back to Pauline. "My God," she whispered. "You're trying to find a way to force me out."

Chapter Ten

"I am not trying to force you out," Pauline insisted. Staring at a spot above and behind Dana's head, she held her body so rigidly she quivered. "All I'm doing is protecting the company."

Dana shifted her glare to Neal. The attorney cringed and whipped a handful of papers behind his back.

What a weasel, she thought. She'd once imagined herself being married to him. Looking past the handsome face, expensive suit and perfectly styled hair, she saw, really saw, the self-centered, opportunistic, shallow creep he actually was.

"By forcing me out with the morals clause?"

The redhead's chin trembled. "Word of your arrest is getting out. Everyone knows you're a suspect. It's a drug dealer, Dana! Five clients have canceled their accounts. Five! Three more wanted to, but I talked them out of it. Good gawd! As far as our clients are concerned, you *are* Star Systems. You're the person they talk to. You solve the problems. Your name is on the letterhead. All this murder crap has everybody running around like chickens in a thunderstorm. Nobody is going to risk their goods with a doped-up killer.''

Dana pressed her arm against her midsection. A bitter flavor filled her mouth. "I didn't kill anybody. I thought you of all people would know that."

"That guy you shot has nothing to do with it. It's—it's the bad publicity. It's the cops poking around and talking to everybody like we're criminals, too. If our clients can't trust us, they'll leave. I'll lose Star Systems." Pauline froze and her eyes widened.

For a long moment, during which Dana imagined the ticking of a loud clock, silence reigned. The guy she shot, she thought dumbly. Her best friend, the person she'd worked side by side with for the past eight years, thought she'd killed a man. Crimson-faced, Pauline stared blindly past Dana. Neal studied his shoes.

Kurt laid a hand on Dana's shoulder.

"I can't deal with this right now," she said. Grit filled her eyes. Her throat hurt. Right at this moment she believed every accusation Carl had made. She even believed Pauline would stoop to hiring Dragon-man.

"It's nothing personal, Dana," Neal said. "The possibility exists that customer files could be subpoenaed and used as evidence. In which case, they'll be part of the public record. Your clients won't risk it. You have a responsibility to protect them as well as yourself."

Pauline turned back to Dana, her face harsh with accusation. "Did you see the story in the paper? Star Systems was named three times. I can't lose everything I've worked for, Dana. I won't. This is my life."

"Let's get out of here," Dana said to Kurt. "I can't deal . . . not now." Her calves burned with the urge to run, but she managed to walk all the way to the elevator.

She punched the down button.

"Dana." Kurt tried to take her arm.

She shrugged him away. "They're ruining me. I haven't done anything, but they're ruining me, anyway." The elevator dinged and the doors slid open. She walked in and stopped in the corner, unable to make herself turn around. If she did, she'd see sympathy on Kurt's face, or worse, pity. "I thought I was innocent until proved guilty. Isn't that how it works?"

"I know you're upset—"

"Don't!" She whirled on him. "Don't say anything nice! I am not upset. I am angry. Furious. Enraged! If I find one shred of proof Pauline is behind all this, I'll strangle her with my bare hands."

He folded his arms and leaned against the stainless steel wall. He cocked an eyebrow.

His sleepy-seeming calm heightened her fury. She shook a fist at him. "They aren't getting way with it. I won't let them."

The car stopped and the doors opened. Dana stalked out. Her heels rang a sharp tattoo, echoing off the concrete walls. Head down, Kurt unlocked the passenger door of his car.

"Well?" she demanded. "Don't you have any smart remarks?"

"I make it a point never to get involved in a temper tantrum." He opened the door and stepped out of range.

She barked a sharp laugh. "This is not a tantrum."

"I didn't say you weren't entitled. I just said I don't get involved." He smiled sweetly.

She flopped onto the seat and clamped her arms over her breasts. "I hate this. It's unfair. It's unjust. They can't do this to me." She wanted to run back upstairs and wave the photographs in Pauline's and Neal's faces. She wanted to see them squirm and turn red-faced and try to deny what the pictures meant.

Kurt maneuvered the big car out of the garage.

She peeked at him and read only concern on his face. The irony of her predicament occurred to her: people she'd known and trusted for years stabbed her in the back, but a man she'd known only a few days was her most staunch supporter. Tears welled in her eyes. She averted her face and blinked rapidly.

"Carl lives in Garland," Kurt said.

"Near Watson Park. Take the expressway to Interstate 635, then get off on Greenville. It's fastest that way." She dug through her purse for a tissue. "When Pauline and I drew up the partnership contract, our lawyer was one of those really cautious types. He put everything in there."

"Including a morals clause."

She dabbed at her burning eyes. "In case one of us went nuts or started drinking up the profits. Do you know anything about contracts? Can she really force me out?"

"I'll look into it."

Dana leaned against the headrest and closed her eyes. "Pauline is so smart. It's amazing what she can do with a computer. She designed our entire system. I

really loved her. I thought she was my best friend."
She turned her head enough to see him. "I'll never be
able to forget this. Even if Carl is wrong about her
stealing, even if the police arrest the real killer and
everything goes back to normal, it'll never be the
same."

He reached across the seat and patted her thigh.
"I'm sorry."

"I thought I knew her." She brought out the
photographs and looked through them. While Neal
had been asking to move in with her, he must have
been seeing Pauline on the side. She felt worse than
sick, she felt utterly stupid. Two-timing jerk—

Kurt turned the wheel, and the big car screamed
around a corner. The force of it flung Dana against the
door. She yelped and flailed wildly for a handhold.
Photographs spilled over her lap and onto the floor.
He stomped the accelerator and sped through an in-
tersection. Tires squealed. Other drivers honked. They
missed hitting a turning truck by inches.

Clutching the armrest for dear life, Dana cried,
"Are you crazy?"

"It's those damned reporters. They must have been
waiting for us at your office building." He glared at
the rearview mirror.

Dana peered over the seat and spotted a red Ford.
"Can we lose them on the expressway?"

"He's not making any attempt to hide. He must
have been waiting outside the garage, hoping to get
lucky. The pinhead."

Dana glared at the Ford, now tailgating them. A
man drove, a woman rode in the passenger seat.

"They want a statement, I'll give them a statement. Stop the car."

"I know you're mad, but talking to them will only make it worse."

She grabbed at the door handle. "I mean it. I'm just in the mood to jump out whether you stop or not."

"I never talk to the press."

"You don't understand. It can't get worse. This is the absolute rock bottom. I am not taking any more. Stop this car!" Yelling felt great. Yelling at the reporters would feel wonderful. Her mouth fairly watered in anticipation.

Kurt pulled into the parking lot of a coffee shop. Before the car even rolled to a complete stop, Dana opened the car door and ripped off her seat belt. "Are you with me or not?"

"As your attorney, I advise against it." He glanced at the Ford, now pulling up behind them. He turned off the ignition.

She bailed out of the car.

The Ford's doors opened and the reporters stepped out. The woman held a tape recorder, the man wielded a video camera. At the rear of the Lincoln, Dana stopped. She leaned against the fender and crossed her arms.

"Ms. Benson," the woman said. "I'm Trudy Ramirez."

"Why are you following me?"

"The public has a right to—"

"I have a right to privacy." She turned her glare on the cameraman. "Turn that thing off. You do not have my permission to film me." Kurt remained in the car and appeared to be talking on a cellular phone. "Turn it off and I'll tell you exactly what happened on Tuesday night."

Trudy and the cameraman exchanged a telling look. Dana could almost see the inner debate, almost smell their eagerness. Trudy held out her hand. "Turn it off, Billy. All right, Ms. Benson, that's all I want. Your side of the story." She pointed her chin at the coffee shop. "Can I buy you lunch?"

"No, thank you." Every day she read the newspaper. On occasional Sundays, she read two or three. She accepted the articles as truth, assuming because they were printed, the journalists had done their jobs and reported the facts. She was media fodder now, and thousands, perhaps millions, would believe what they read about her.

Kurt opened the car door and ambled over to Dana's side. He gave her a grin and a wink. "I'm Kurt Saxon, Ms. Benson's attorney." He was up to something.

Trudy gave Kurt a sweet-as-syrup smile. "I know you. Your client has agreed to an interview." She handed her tape recorder to the cameraman and brought out a notebook. "Are you sure you don't want to go inside? The traffic is loud. We can talk over a cup of coffee.

"We'll stay right here," Kurt said.

Trudy narrowed her eyes and chewed her lower lip. "This isn't a war, Ms. Benson. We aren't enemies. I just want to hear your side of the story."

Dana didn't believe this woman with her sharp eyes and aggressive posture held even a smidgen of sympathy. "Fine, I'll tell you what happened to me on Tuesday."

"First things first. Theodore Gordon is a known drug dealer. He's got a long criminal history. I've talked to some people who know you, done my research. Nothing indicates you use illicit drugs. How is it you know the deceased?"

"I don't know him."

"The police dropped the arrest warrant. Is this a case of self-defense? Were you being robbed?" Her gaze lingered on Dana's bruised arms. "Attempted rape?"

Talk about loaded questions. If she denied being attacked, then she sounded like a cold-blooded murderer. Dana began to regret her impulsive behavior. She should have listened to Kurt. "I'll tell you what happened on Tuesday. Do you want my side of it or not?"

"I'm listening."

"All right in a nutshell, then. I went to work that day. Nothing was going on, so around five-thirty I went home. I ate some chicken salad and drank iced tea. I pulled some weeds out of my flower bed. I vacuumed the carpeting. I called my mother and we chatted about the weather. I read the newspaper and a few chapters of a novel. Then I went to bed. And I stayed there."

Trudy wrote furiously. Her pen hand stilled. She blinked several times and lifted her head. Anger furrowed her forehead. "What is this?"

"I didn't go to O'Dooley's. I didn't kill anyone. It's a case of mistaken identity."

"Witnesses claim there's a videotape of you committing the murder, Ms. Benson. No one has any doubts about your identity. I happen to know you participated in a lineup and several witnesses identified you."

"They're mistaken. It isn't me." She dropped her arms to her sides and took a step closer to the reporter. "I don't know if you've ever been falsely accused of anything, Ms. Ramirez. It's an ugly situation I wouldn't wish upon my worst enemy. All of a sudden, my honesty doesn't matter, my reputation doesn't matter. I don't matter."

"So you're denying the police have cause to suspect you."

Dana could have groaned. Trudy wasn't buying any of it. "Of course I'm denying it. I don't know what happened at O'Dooley's because I was not there. I have nothing to tell you. Now, please, leave me alone."

"Let me get this straight, then," Trudy said. "You deny knowing Gordon. Never seen him before."

"That's right."

"Can you explain why the police found his fingerprints in your business office?"

Dana gasped. Kurt seemed to swell. Dana eyed him questioningly, but his expression offered no explanations for this revelation.

Quick as a duck on a bug, Trudy picked up on their reactions. "It's true! You do know the victim, Ms. Benson. I've checked out Star Systems. I wouldn't call Gordon your type of client."

Kurt said, "Your source is mistaken."

Smiling, shaking her head, Trudy wagged her pen at Kurt. I caught you, her expression said.

I'm sorry, Dana told him with her eyes, you were right, I shouldn't have started this. What do I do now?

"You've got quite a reputation around the courthouse, Mr. Saxon. Your clients are drug dealers, burglars, muggers, the dirtiest cases. If Ms. Benson isn't guilty, why did she hire you?"

A man on a motorcycle roared into the parking lot. The big machine growled, making the air vibrate. Chrome glittered in the sunlight. Two more men on equally large bikes pulled in after him. People leaving the coffee shop eyed the trio. Women held their purses closer to their sides.

Kurt took Dana's arm and said, "Cavalry's here." To the reporters he spoke louder. "Interview's over, folks. If you'll excuse us."

The bikers, large, filthy, hairy and menacing, surrounded the red Ford. One parked behind the car, the other two pulled in front. The riders revved their engines, creating a blatting, exhaust-tinged, stereo roar. Trudy and the cameraman edged closer together.

"You also have a reputation as a real smart aleck, Saxon," Trudy called. "Is this your idea of a joke?"

Dana slid into the Lincoln. She whispered, "Who are those men?" Wearing leather jackets and ripped jeans stained by grease and road dust, the bikers looked dangerous.

"Former clients. They owed me a favor," Kurt replied. "They hang out at a bar about a mile from here." His smile faded. "Ms. Ramirez is right, my clients are scum. Does that bother you?"

She considered it. At least she now knew why Neal had found Kurt for her. Neal thought her guilty. "Do you think I'm scum?"

"Not in the least."

"Then, no, it doesn't bother me."

Within a minute he was driving out of the parking lot, leaving the reporters blocked in by the glowering outlaws. Dana watched until they were out of sight.

"They won't . . . hurt anybody, will they?"

"Nah. They're just having a good time." He picked up the envelope. "Gather up the pictures. We're taking this to the cops."

"What for?"

"Gordon's fingerprints." He tossed the envelope on her lap. "This is not good, babe."

"We have to talk to Carl first."

"The cops will talk to Carl."

"We don't know this is what Dragon-man wants. Let's talk to Carl first and find out what's going on."

"If he tells you he doesn't have anything to do with Dragon-man, you'll believe him."

Despite wishful thinking, she knew in her heart her former bookkeeper had something to do with the murder and Dragon-man. She noticed Kurt was headed south, toward downtown Dallas and the police station. "Please turn around. Carl should be home. It won't take that much time. If he's not there, then we'll go to the police."

He drove a few blocks, then smacked the turn indicator. He pulled into a gas station and swung around the pump island. At the driveway entrance, he glowered at traffic.

Pleased he'd listened to her for once, she said, "He's my friend. I want to hear what he has to say."

"I'm not overly impressed with your friends."

She winced and gathered the fallen photographs.

"There's such a thing as being too good, too trusting. You're a nice person, so you assume everyone else is just as nice."

"Not necessarily," she murmured.

"If he were your friend, he'd have warned you about Dragon-man."

Tangled emotions made her entire body ache. "If we give the pictures to the police, what are they going to do? The only thing they prove is Pauline's bad taste."

Muttering a curse, he pulled into traffic.

When they reached the condominium complex where Carl lived, Kurt shut off the car and rested his forearms on the steering wheel. "We're not here because I think Carl is a swell guy. But damn it, you're right. Those pictures are nothing without Carl. If the cops don't laugh at our faces, they'll laugh at our backs." He turned his head just enough to see her.

His expression frightened her. She swallowed the hard lump in her throat.

"I've got a feeling Carl isn't here. It's bugging me, him not contacting you. He has to know what happened at O'Dooley's."

The lump increased to choking proportions. "Maybe he thinks I shot Gordon."

"Whatever. Let's go."

"What is it? You are scaring me to death. What are you thinking?"

"I'm thinking Dragon-man didn't ask nice for the pictures."

That was a fear she'd been shoving away ever since she saw the envelope contained photographs. "We won't find out by sitting in your car." She opened the door.

Carl lived in a small garden apartment surrounded by a cutwork cinder-block wall. They entered the garden through a black wrought-iron gate. She noticed the newspapers piled around the door. Several were gray and warped from being rained upon.

"Looks like he's gone on vacation," Kurt said, and pressed the bell.

Dana shook her head. "Carl is one of those compulsive planners. He'd have canceled the newspaper. Dragon-man must have..." She did not dare say aloud what she was thinking.

Kurt rapped his knuckles against the door. He waited, then used his fist. The sound echoed inside the small garden patio. Dana used her shoe to roll over a soggy newspaper. Pill bugs scurried for cover. Kurt tried the doorknob—it was unlocked. The door squeaked on the hinges.

Dana's mouth went dry and she shook her head. She whispered, "You are not going in there! It's private property and you can't!"

"He might be sick. Or have a broken leg and can't reach the phone to call for help."

"Now you're being ridiculous. You said yourself he's not home." She caught his arm and dug her fingers into his leather jacket sleeve. Fear clawed its way up her throat. "We weren't invited and we are not going in there. That is that! We can talk to his neighbors. Maybe one of them knows where Carl is.''

''I'll just pop in and pop out.'' He shook his arm; she tightened her hold. ''I won't touch anything.''

''Please stop this.'' Denial failed her; Carl was dead. She knew it, she felt it. He was lying on the floor, shot or stabbed, bloody and stiff. ''Let's call the police. Right now.''

Kurt stuck his head inside the apartment. ''Oh, man.''

Horrified, Dana backed away and clapped her hands over her mouth. She watched Kurt take a cautious step inside.

STANDING STOCK-STILL, Kurt surveyed the damage in the apartment. Pictures ripped off the wall, lamps and furniture broken, sofa cushions slashed, carpeting torn up from the floor. He whistled soft and low. All doubts about Carl's involvement with Dragon-man wisped away.

''Is he dead?'' Dana whispered from the doorway.

Her shoulder and one foot were visible. His heart ached for her. ''I don't think so. We'd smell a body.''

She peeked around the door. Her eyes widened into shocked blue moons. ''Good heavens.''

''Come in, but don't touch anything.'' He waited until she crept inside.

She held herself so tightly she practically stood on one foot. ''Carl's the one, isn't he? Dragon-man looked here, too.''

''Afraid so. Don't move.'' He made his careful way over the scattered papers and broken glass. There was one bedroom, and it had been destroyed as savagely as the living room. This wasn't the result of a mere search. This was the work of a sick, furious mind bent on total destruction.

One corner of the room had the looks of an office. A computer monitor lay shattered on the floor. The computer itself had been wrenched open and the boards inside ripped out and broken. Major overkill.

"Kurt? Oh, Kurt, come look."

He hurried back to the living room. Dana, her face so pale it had a bluish cast, pointed a shaking finger at the floor. He examined the rusty-black splotches and streaks on the beige carpet.

"Is that what I think it is?"

He looked up at her. "It's blood, but there's not much. I don't think—" Shredded strips of silver duct tape caught his attention. A lot of tape was scattered around. He carefully lifted a piece.

Dark hairs clung to the tape. "What does Carl look like?"

"He's fairly small. About five foot six, thin. He eats and eats but never gains weight. He has hair about your color, maybe a little lighter. He wears it short. And he wears glasses."

Kurt found a penknife. It was cheap, with a red plastic cover and had a small chain attached for hanging on a key ring. The tiny blade was broken in half. He grinned. "Old Carl gave Dragon-man the slip." He dangled the tape strip for her to see. "There's enough tape here to tie up an orchestra, except Carl got his hands on a knife."

Hope brought color back to her cheeks. "Then he's alive?"

"Any idea where he'd go? Where he'd hide out?"

"Not really. He never had many friends. He has no family."

Kurt turned in a slow circle, trying to get a feel for the events. An overturned bowl and moldering cereal and milk on the counter said the attack had probably come while Carl was eating breakfast. He'd answered the door and Dragon-man had shoved his way inside. Blood indicated injuries, but Carl hadn't been so badly hurt he couldn't use a miniature penknife to saw through duct tape.

He spotted a photo album lying open on the floor. Photographs, each neatly marked with a caption and date, were encased in plastic sleeves. Several of the pictures were of Dana. "Dana and the duck"; "Dana, world-class diver"; "Dana and the first fish of the day."

"Look at this," she said. Her hand hovered over the spilled contents of a file folder. "This is Pauline's."

Kurt crouched and poked through receipts, credit-card slips, bills and letters. He lifted a letter from a collection agency. Coffee stains on the paper made him grin. Old Carl had done some garbage collecting.

He began to get a sense of the man, unused to adventure or excitement, but determined. Tailing Pauline, pawing through her trash, doggedly seeking the evidence he needed to redeem himself in Dana's eyes.

He sympathized. Dana was the kind of woman for whom a man would go to the ends of the earth.

"Is this the proof Carl meant?"

"Must be. Looks like Pauline has some financial problems. Are you aware of it?"

"I know she's always complaining about money. I didn't know it was this bad. This bill is for more than a thousand dollars."

"Looks like her debt goes a lot deeper than that." He sat back on his heels, puzzling over what this might mean. If Pauline hired Dragon-man to retrieve evidence of her perfidy, why leave all this behind? "I'm getting mixed messages."

"We better call the police—aack!"

Kurt looked over his shoulder. Every hair on his head leapt to attention and his heart dropped into his belly. A man had his arm around Dana's throat. He pressed the business end of a nine-millimeter pistol against her ear.

Dana's eyes rolled wildly. Kurt stared at the man's trigger finger.

"Get your hands up where I can see them. Any tricks and I'm gonna show Dana here how mad I am about her icing my buddy."

Chapter Eleven

On his knees, with his hands clamped firmly on his head, Kurt called himself fifty kinds of jackass. Stupid, stupid, not to consider the goof might be lying in wait for them. Even stupider, after leaving his gun in the car before visiting Dana's office, he'd neglected to strap it back on.

Some bodyguard.

Dana sat on a shredded couch cushion. She laced her fingers atop her head and never took her eyes off Dragon-man. Sweat gave her pale face a sheen. She kept licking her lips. Kurt tried to communicate with his eyes. All he needed was the goof's attention off Dana for a second. One second.

"All right, boys and girls, let's try this again," Dragon-man said. "Where are the pictures, Dana?"

"There are no pictures," Kurt said. "Carl lied to you."

"Shut up. Didn't give you leave to speak." Dragon-man peered suspiciously at Kurt. "You a private dick or something?"

About forty, Dragon-man had a broad, flat face, ruddy and freckled. Sandy hair shot through with gray was buzz-cut close to his skull. He held a nine-millimeter semiautomatic pistol with ease borne of long familiarity. His knuckles were tattooed with crude black letters, Love on his right hand, Hate on his left. His narrow eyes were as soulless as a shark's.

Kurt tried to place his accent. It was southern, but not Texan. Definitely backwoods.

Definitely dangerous.

"I'm a circus clown," Kurt said. "I'm always looking for idiots. Want a job?"

In two long strides he was at Kurt's side. Kurt braced himself, every muscle straining. Even knowing it was coming didn't help. A flash of steel and it felt as if his face exploded. Gray mist blurred his vision. White-hot sparks exploded in his brain.

Dana screamed.

Stunned, Kurt toppled to his side. The world spun furiously and fireworks exploded behind his closed eyelids. Soft hands fluttered over his face.

"You hurt him! He's bleeding! Don't hit him again. I'll give you the pictures, don't hurt him."

"Always a weak link," Dragon-man said. "You be big a chicken as your little buddy."

Kurt kept his eyes closed, listening to the iron-shod hooves thundering through his skull. Dana ran her hands through his hair and her fingers fluttered over his forehead. Kurt wanted to tell her it wasn't serious, head wounds always bled more than the injury warranted. But he played dead.

He needed an opening.

"Oh, Kurt, I am so sorry. Wake up, can you hear me?"

"That's right, cooperate now. Make ya a deal, you tell me where the pictures are and I don't put no bullets in the clown's head. How 'bout that, huh?"

Kurt listened to shuffling feet and Dana's protests. Her hands left his face. Kurt breathed deeply, listening intently. He pushed away the pain in his head, setting it aside, freeing his concentration. Couch springs squeaked. Dana grunted.

Dragon-man demanded, "Let's hear you sing."

"They're in Kurt's car. On the front seat in an envelope. Take them. Just don't hurt him anymore. Please."

Kurt risked opening one eye. As he'd hoped, Dragon-man was facing Dana, the gun was lowered, and his legs were within range. He kicked with his left leg, hard and fast, catching the other man below the knees. Dragon-man yowled. He crashed to the floor.

Kurt followed through, rolling to his hands and knees. He kicked again, pistoning his leg, relishing the solid connection and Dragon-man's howl of pain and rage. The man smashed into a fallen chair and wood splintered. The pistol went flying into the kitchen, skittering across the linoleum floor.

"Run!" he yelled at Dana. "Get the hell out of here! Go, go!"

Kurt grabbed at Dragon-man, but he slithered away, scrambling to his feet. He swung wildly, grazing Kurt's jaw, then jumped back.

Dana screamed, "Don't move or I'll shoot!" She stood in the small dining area, her feet planted in a wide stance and both hands on the pistol.

Dragon-man froze, quivering.

"I swear, I'll kill you. Get away, go away."

Never taking his eyes off Dragon-man, Kurt got to his feet. "Give me the gun, babe."

Dragon-man bolted. He tore open the door and raced out, hitting the gate with a clatter. Kurt grabbed the gun out of Dana's hands.

A sudden wave of dizziness made the room spin. He lurched off-balance, momentarily blind. As if through a wall of water, he heard Dana cry out his name. He dropped to one knee. Then her arms were around him and she pressed his cheek against her soft bosom.

"I'm all right," he said thickly.

"You're bleeding. I have to get you to a hospital." She helped him upright.

His legs wobbled. His eyes kept watering and he felt the pulsing tautness across his forehead.

He blinked blood out of his eyes and checked the piece. It was cheap and cruddy-looking, dirty and probably as dangerous to its owner as to the target. He checked the load and found a full clip of nine-millimeter rounds. He told Dana to gather up the folder Carl had assembled about Pauline.

She did so, then put her arm around his waist and steadied him as they left the apartment.

A woman walking a poodle took one look at them and scooped her little dog into her arms. She scurried away. Kurt knew he should ask around to see if anyone had witnessed Dragon-man's escape, but his head hurt.

"We have to call the police." Dana looked around fearfully.

"Uh-uh, can't deal with the cops right now, hospital first." Kurt dug into his pocket for his keys. "Here, you drive."

"YOU'RE A LUCKY MAN, no concussion." Austin peered at Kurt's battered face with open interest and a touch of admiration.

"Yeah, yeah," Kurt said, waving him away. He'd spent three hours waiting in the emergency room so the doctor could spend ten minutes putting two stitches in his forehead. Since they'd returned to Dana's home, the pain had subsided to manageable proportions, but his mood hadn't improved a bit.

Snooky was finding the smell of antiseptic intriguing. He tried to lick the wound. Kurt lifted the cat off the back of the couch and set him on the floor. "Beat it, you ghoul," he growled. Snooky gave him a glare before strolling away.

"Yet another battle scar to impress the ladies," Austin said. "Cool. A few more of those and you'll catch up to me." His smile turned grim. "You're sure these are the pictures Dragon-man wants?"

"Yeah, I'm sure, but hell if I know why."

Dana appeared, bearing a glass of water, a bottle of pain relievers and an ice pack. "Put this on the swelling."

"You can quit babying me any time now." He swallowed three tablets and drained the water glass.

Dana had changed her bloodied sweater and slacks for a sweat suit. Her face was scrubbed, and she smelled of soap and freshness. Her sweet scent and deep concern made him feel better. A little. It helped ease the lingering fear of seeing her with a gun to her head. A lot. She placed the ice pack gently against the wound. "I can't believe the police are making us wait."

"Callister and Tannenbaum are investigating a crime scene for another homicide. I left a message for them. I don't want to talk to anyone else."

"Humph. They're putting us off because they don't believe us. I know that's what it is. They think we're making the whole thing up."

"They'll be here eventually."

"Before or after Dragon-man kills me? Or you?"

"I screwed up. I'm sorry, but it won't happen again. You're safe. Everything is okay now."

Austin cleared his throat. "Can you two discuss this later? I have things to do. What do you figure happened to Carl?" He leafed through the photographs and read Carl's plaintive note.

Dana explained, "I fired Carl because I thought he'd embezzled from the company. I think I was wrong."

The ice pack felt good. Kurt closed his eyes, savoring the spreading numbness. "So Carl snapped some pictures of Pauline and Neal Harlow. He mails the pictures to Dana as proof that Pauline is messing around with Dana's boyfriend."

"Neal is not my boyfriend," she said testily.

"It looks like Dragon-man and his buddy Eddie jumped Carl and took the original pictures. They beat the hell out of him until he told them he sent a set of duplicates to Dana."

"Any idea why?" Austin asked.

"It's possible Pauline found out about Carl's surveillance and hired the goofs."

"I just can't believe that," Dana said. She indicated the folder full of receipts and dunning notices. "It's like you said, why get excited about the pictures but leave this?"

Kurt chewed it over. "Only Carl knows."

Dana looked troubled. "I wonder if Carl thinks Pauline and I are in it together. That could be why he hasn't contacted me."

The angle made sense. Carl mailed the photos, expecting Dana to contact him after two or three days, but the mail got held up. Then he's jumped by a pair of goofs. So he thinks Dana talked to Pauline, which made Dana the enemy.

"None of which gets us any closer to Dana's double or how she figures into this mess."

"That may change. I learned a few things." Austin leaned back on the chair and hooked his hands behind his neck. "One of the waitresses at O'Dooley's said when the bartender showed her the photo of Dana in the newspaper, she was sure Dana wasn't the woman."

Kurt forgot about his aching head. Dana shifted on the couch so she could hold the ice pack and watch the private eye.

Austin brushed a hand across his shoulder-length hair. "She thinks the woman had short hair. Trouble is, the woman was wearing a jacket and never took it off, so her hair might have been tucked inside."

"The little discrepancies are adding up." Kurt grasped Dana's wrist and moved her hand and the ice pack to a more comfortable position. He could hold the ice himself, but it felt better when she did it.

"We might find an even bigger discrepancy. I think there's a witness who saw the actual shooting."

Kurt drew Dana's hand away from his head, but kept his hold on her wrist. "A reliable witness?"

"Don't know yet. Her name is Patty Cartwell. She's a bartender. She was on break, fooling around with her boyfriend out in the parking lot."

"Did she talk to you?"

Austin grinned that secretive smile of his. "She avoided me, and she's avoiding the police. I think she saw something."

"What about her boyfriend?"

"He's the reason she doesn't want to get involved. He's married. Talking to the police means admitting he was with Patty. His wife won't approve."

Kurt kept his cussing to himself, barely. "What's his name?"

"Bob. That's all I have right now."

"This is good. You keep working on the double, I'll see what I can do about Patty and Bob."

"If they did see the shooting, can we force them to talk to the police?" Dana asked.

Kurt entwined his fingers with hers and squeezed. "We'll play it by ear. Could be, we don't want them talking to the police." He gave her a reassuring smile. "What's your next step, man?"

"I'm still working on the first step. I figure our mystery lady picked O'Dooley's for a reason. It can't be convenience to where you work, Dana. It's four miles from your office building and almost eight miles from here. So she probably has a room or an apartment nearby." He rose and picked up his jacket. "Need anything else?"

"Make me some copies of those pictures. I don't want to give them up to the cops until I know what they mean. Thanks for coming through for me, man. You do good work."

"That's what friends are for." He tucked the pictures in his jacket pocket. "I'll have them for you tomorrow. I can stay tonight, if you want."

"I'll call if I need you."

Dana saw the private eye out. She rejoined Kurt on the couch and regarded him gravely. "Dragon-man will be back."

He laid his hand along her cheek. "You handled yourself good today. You didn't panic."

She leaned into his caress. "I've never been so scared in my life. I thought he'd killed you." Soft color rose in her cheeks. "I've only known you a few days, but we've been through so much and—and—"

His mood vastly improved. "You care about me."

She nodded and smiled, her eyes downcast. "I do."

He grasped the back of her neck and eased her toward him. Kissing her made the pain in his head go away. Her lips were soft as velvet; her response fired his blood. Nordic coloring aside, she was no ice princess.

She broke away abruptly. For a moment he held her, but her tension made him withdraw his hands.

"What's the matter?" he asked.

She shook her head and stood up. "I do care about you, Kurt, and I think we can be friends. But I don't want to do anything we'll regret."

Hot arousal made his groin ache. He'd never in his life wanted a woman the way he wanted her. "I won't regret anything. Trust me."

"I am so very grateful. You saved my life." She backed slowly around the couch. "You're a wonderful man, you're amazing, but...gratitude isn't enough for me. You're sexy and...well, you're sexy, but we shouldn't get involved. Not that way. We're just not compatible, and a casual affair isn't..."

He snatched up the ice pack and jammed it against his head. The sharp pain took his mind off other bodily aches, but the pain in his heart thumped and thudded. "I get it. I'm good enough to rescue you but not good enough to sleep with. Just not classy enough for a high-toned lady like you. But hey, don't worry, I know my place. Your precious virtue's safe with me."

Her expression went frosty and her back stiffened. "You must be hungry. I'll fix you a sandwich." Without awaiting his reply, she went to the kitchen.

Had words that stupid actually come from his mouth? Pressing the ice pack to his head, he closed his eyes.

DANA PEERED THROUGH the open French doors into the dining room where Kurt had set up a makeshift office. He'd appropriated her computer. At the moment he was typing and scowling at his notes.

All day she'd been avoiding him. Her rejection had hurt his feelings; his nasty comment had hurt hers. She wanted to apologize, but didn't know how. Or for what exactly. She'd meant what she said. She couldn't sleep with him out of gratitude, or because Dragonman frightened her, or because her life was turned upside down and a warm body would be a distraction.

She cared about Kurt Saxon, but caring wasn't enough, either. She needed love and commitment, stability and order.

Sighing, she studied her formerly formal dining room. Domestically, Kurt was a disaster. He'd surrounded himself with a bulwark of stacked files and books. How he could possibly find anything, she hadn't a clue.

He noticed her. "Do you need something?"

She needed to explain herself better. She needed to apologize. She needed to figure out why her mind accepted his unsuitability, but her heart and body engaged in open rebellion. "How does your head feel?"

He rubbed his eyes with the pads of his fingers. "Need glasses. I'm getting old."

"I meant the cut, Kurt."

"I heal fast." He typed in a few commands to save and close the files. He turned off the computer and checked his watch. "I guess Callister and Tannenbaum won't contact us today. It's late and I'm starving."

Despite his messiness, he could cook. For dinner he concocted a mixture of marinated flank steak and vegetables over steamed rice that was better than anything she'd ever eaten in a Chinese restaurant.

Dana picked at her food. She wished he would talk to her. He wasn't exactly giving her the cold shoulder but he wasn't exactly friendly, either. He slumped on the couch with his feet up on the coffee table. A glass of iced tea was set two inches away from the coaster Dana had provided. He used the television remote to surf between a soccer game, a home-improvement program about installing drywall and Congressional hearings.

And he fed the cat off his plate.

Men and women, she thought glumly. They may as well be different species considering how well they communicated. "When are we going to talk to the bartender and see if she saw the shooting?"

"We'll catch her at work." He changed the channel again.

He definitely was ignoring her. Men!

She placed his sweating iced-tea glass on the coaster and used her sleeve to wipe the ring off the wood. "How you survive as a bachelor I will never know."

Gaze fixed on the television, he said, "Huh?"

"I have been picking up after you all day. You're putting water rings on the furniture. You leave the cordless phone all over the house, and I am sick and tired of looking for it. And I keep tripping over the cat!"

He pulled an offended face and turned to Snooky. "Is she talking to us? Hey, I shower every day. Change my underwear."

"I didn't say you were dirty, I said you're a mess. You've been in my house two days and the place looks as if fourteen children live here." She tossed a glare at the dumbbells he'd left in a corner. "Who finds the telephone for you when I'm not around?"

"Are you offering to take care of me?"

He smiled broadly, showing his teeth, and his eyes sparkled with bright amusement. As the warmth of his smile embraced her, her irritation faded.

She escaped into the kitchen and began tackling the dirty dishes. Don't think about him, she counseled herself. Don't look at him and don't pick quarrels.

"Oh, princess," Kurt said in a goofy voice. He danced Dopey, her Disney dwarf doll, on the countertop. "Kurt says he's sorry for being a slob."

She tried not to smile. "That is not a toy. Put it away."

"Looks like a toy." He flopped the doll back and forth.

She opened the dishwasher to load it. "I'm sorry I snapped at you."

He made the doll stand on its head and wiggled its feet. "You're right. My secretary gives me hell constantly for misplacing things and never washing my coffee cup."

"Ick."

"Fungus is flavor, that's what I always say." He propped Dopey atop a telephone book. "Go on, I'll clean the kitchen."

"It's all right. You cooked." She looked at him sideways. "It was very good. Thank you."

He came around the counter, anyway, and started water running in the sink. They worked in silence, with Kurt scrubbing pots and Dana drying. Snooky wanted to leap up on the counters and scrounge for leftovers. Dana kept chasing him away, but the cat turned her efforts into a game. He'd jump on a counter until she yelled at him, then fluff his tail and scamper away. He sneaked around on the floor and darted at her, batting her ankles with his big, soft paws.

Kurt was rooting for the cat.

She shook a finger at him. "That animal would be much better behaved if you treated him like a cat instead of a person."

"I don't treat him like a person." He dried his hands.

"Then train him not to walk on the counters."

Snooky jumped onto a stool and placed his paws on the counter, prepared to launch.

"Hey, you heard the lady," Kurt said. "Get your hands off."

Dana laughed. "I give up. You're both impossible."

Kurt took her upper arm in a gentle grip. "I'll try to keep my stuff out of your way."

She wished he wouldn't look at her the way he looked at her now. When those pale gray eyes focused so intently on her, the rest of the world faded into mist. Her heart rate increased, breathing became a conscious endeavor. She felt all wobbly inside.

She didn't want to think about how good he smelled. Or how his size made her feel fragile and feminine. His bandaged forehead reminded her of how terrifying their experience with Dragon-man had been, and the worst part had been seeing him lying so still and bleeding.

He canted his head slightly. His lips parted. He was going to kiss her. She dragged her eyes away. "Austin told me you're divorced."

He narrowed his eyes and leaned against the counter, resting his big hands over the rim. "He did, did he?"

"Is it a sore subject?" Shut up, she told herself. This was not a safe conversation. It made her sound too interested.

"Not particularly." His smile challenged her. "We were married eight years, have been divorced five. No kids. We got married because I thought she was the sexiest girl in the world and she thought I was a hot-shot attorney who'd be a millionaire before I was thirty. We were both wrong. She got the house, cars and bank accounts. I got some peace and quiet. So everybody's happy. You want to know anything else?"

"No." Saying no felt as uncomfortable as a lie.

"So what about you? Why aren't you married?"

"That's not the kind of question a gentleman asks a lady."

He glanced at the Dopey doll. "I knew it. You're waiting to be swept away by a white knight on a fiery charger."

"Stop teasing me about my hobby. Fairy tales are a pastime, not something I believe in."

"Don't get so defensive. I'm just curious." His smile faded and he crossed his arms. He stared at the floor. "About last night. I stepped way out of line. I shouldn't have said what I said. I'm sorry."

"It's my fault for leading you on," she said carefully. "Relationships are too important to take lightly. I find you attractive and—"

"Then I stand a chance with you."

"I suppose it depends upon your intentions."

She met his eyes and held his gaze. She did want him sexually. He was the most exciting man she'd ever met. He was warm and funny, generous and confident.

If she stepped over the line into the promise of his eyes, she'd fall in love.

He pushed away from the counter and strolled past her. Hands behind his back, he wandered to the doors facing the backyard. "I could fall for you, Dana, hard and fast, full of fireworks. It's like you stepped right out of my dreams."

Her sentiments exactly. Knowing there was more, she chewed her lower lip.

"You know that old saying about getting right back in the saddle after you've been bucked off a horse? It's a load of crap. I got bucked off a horse once. Only that wasn't good enough for the horse. He turned around and stomped me, caved in a couple ribs." He tapped his chest with a finger. "Me, I'm not stupid. There isn't enough money in the world to get me on top of a horse again." He smiled, but it failed to reach his eyes. "It's only fair to warn you, marriage is the same thing."

She laughed uncertainly. "I'm not asking you to marry me."

"I mean it, I could fall for you in the worst kind of way. I'll treat you good, make love to you until your eyes turn color. But if you're aiming for a ring and a license..." He slowly shook his head. "That's a saddle I'm never climbing into again."

This was what she needed to know, wanted to know. He had no interest in commitments, she had no interest in a casual affair. So each of them knew where the other stood.

But it hurt, anyway. "Thank you for your honesty."

The doorbell chimed.

"That'll be Austin with the pictures," he said. "He's going to spend the night on the couch. I'm worn-out, so he'll be another set of ears in case Dragon-man decides to make a move."

"We haven't finished this discussion."

"We have unless one of us is willing to compromise."

Score one for him; the ball was squarely in her court. "It won't be me, Kurt."

He exhaled heavily. "Whatever."

TANGLED IN HER THOUGHTS, Dana lay in bed, staring at the ceiling. Despite Kurt in the spare bedroom and Austin in the family room, she'd spent another restless night, listening to creaks, bumps, groans and scratchy noises, wondering if Dragon-man was going to sneak into her house and kill her.

A heavy fist pounded on her bedroom door. Kurt poked his head inside. "You awake?"

She snatched bed coverings over her breasts. "Do you mind?"

"Not at all." To her astonishment, he walked in. The man acted as if he owned the place. His darned cat did, too. Snooky strolled in behind Kurt and had the audacity to jump up on her bed.

"It's almost noon. No more lazing around. Up, up." He clapped his hands. "Tannenbaum called. He and Callister decided they have time to chat."

She'd known it was late, but noon? She glanced at the nightstand. Her clock radio was missing.

Following her gaze, he said, "I borrowed your radio. I like music when I work. Hope you don't mind."

He'd snuck in here while she slept and stole her radio and he expected her not to mind?

"Hey, it's not like I peeked under the covers." He craned his neck, looking with open interest at her bare shoulders. "Do you wear PJs?"

"Get out!" She snatched up a pillow and threw it at him. It went *flump* against his face. "Out!"

Kurt and the cat made a hasty departure.

After she dressed, she hurried downstairs and stomped into the kitchen. "We're going to have a little discussion about privacy—"

With the phone lodged against his ear, he waved a hand for her to be quiet. He pointed to the cup of coffee poured and ready for her. Glowering and grumbling over his high-handedness, she focused on her coffee. Rules, that's what she needed. Rule number one, her bedroom was strictly off limits. Number two, he would pick up after himself. Number three, the cat stayed off the furniture.

He hung up and tossed the phone on the counter. His broad face fairly gleamed. Without warning, he caught her face in both hands and kissed her soundly on the mouth. A warm, smacking, heart-pounding kiss that knocked her hastily composed rules right out of her head.

"That was Austin. He's got a solid lead on your double."

Chapter Twelve

"A lead?" Dana whispered. "She actually exists?"

"Hell, yes, she exists. You had doubts?" Kurt held her shoulders. Smiling the way he smiled now, with his broad craggy face inner-lit and glowing, he was beautiful.

"She's a phantom wearing my face, popping in to ruin my life and popping out again. Disappearing into thin air." She gulped in a steadying breath. "What kind of lead? Has he actually seen her?"

"He showed your picture to a mechanic. The guy replaced a muffler, and he's positive about his identification of the owner. Not only that, but the woman has short hair, just like the one the waitress described. That's solid corroboration."

"She exists."

"She paid cash, so he doesn't have a name, but he did record the license plate number. Not only that, but the mechanic is willing to talk to the police. We've got her, babe."

She could kiss him. Emotion nearly as strong as the fear and shocks of the past few days filled her, tightened her chest. She raised her hands to his hands and caressed his weathered knuckles, exploring his strength.

"Happy?" he asked.

"Very."

"We're not out of the woods yet. We still have to convince the cops it was her and not you. We still have to explain Eddie Gordon's fingerprints in your office."

"We'll find Carl." She traced the heavy knobs of bone in his wrists.

When he kissed her, she was ready for him, meeting him more than halfway. She slid her hands up his arms, delighting in the sensation of rock-solid muscle under the smooth cotton of his shirt. He wrapped her in his embrace, pressing her body against his, thigh-to-thigh, belly-to-belly. He kissed her with raw and honest hunger, his thrusting tongue claiming and possessing hers. She worked her fingers through his hair, finding it soft and heavy.

Desire burned, swelling. Each touch, from him sliding his hand down her spine to the delicious sensation of him exploring the tender nape of her neck, fueled the inner fires. Her breasts grew heavy, straining against the lace on her bra, aching for a touch. She flattened them against his chest, reveling in his vibrancy and the heat searing through their clothes.

He broke the kiss gently, nibbling on her lower lip.

She savored the rain-fresh taste of him, now forever branded in her brain. "Oh, no," she breathed. "Don't do this."

His eyes mesmerized her. His brash manner challenged her. For a man like him, nothing was impossible.

It was easy to imagine waking up to his face every day.

Until the day another fantasy woman caught his fancy. Until he decided to leave.

With a rueful laugh, he turned her loose. "Oh, yeah, forgot about our differing viewpoints. Ready to compromise?"

"Are you?"

"Guess not." He opened the oven. "Sit down. I made you a waffle."

His answer dismayed her. Did her answer matter to him at all? Probably not. A man like him probably had dozens of women willing to settle for a slice of his attention. "I have a waffle iron?"

"It's mine." He produced a waffle from inside the oven, put it on a plate and sprinkled it with a dusting of powdered sugar. With a flourish, he set it before her.

She arched an eyebrow. "Are you trying to seduce me with food?"

"Will it work?" He fetched a small saucepan from the stove. He spooned strawberry compote over her waffle.

She eyed the golden waffle and glistening red fruit. It smelled heavenly. "I doubt it." It tasted heavenly, too.

He glanced at the cabinet holding her medieval figurines. "Food's not the only trick in my repertoire. I think you need poetry." He waggled his eyebrows.

"You need somebody willing to fight duels, sweep you away, maybe ravish you a little bit."

"Ravish me?" She squirmed against the sudden tingling in her upper thighs. That he seemed to read her deepest fantasies was strangely erotic, but at the same time disconcerting. She forced a laugh. "I don't need ravishing. I'm not interested in silly games."

He put the saucepan on a trivet. He tapped his chin in a thoughtful manner. "If you want to be a stick in the mud, the offer of dinner is still open."

"Is that with or without ravishment?"

"Your choice," he promised in a velvet voice.

Quit, she told herself. She wasn't right for him, he wasn't right for her. They'd already established that. End of story. "I'll think about it."

The doorbell rang.

Kurt checked his watch. "They got here fast." He huffed a sharp breath. "Are you ready?"

"I suppose," she said with a sigh. Even with proof the other woman existed, facing the police was not going to be fun. Especially Detective Callister with his skepticism and hostility.

"We tell them everything."

"I have nothing to hide. I just want this over with."

He went to answer the door. He soon returned, but instead of the police, her parents, their faces gray with fatigue and concern, accompanied Kurt.

Dana nearly fell off the stool.

WHAT KURT READ on Dana's face could only be described as pure panic.

"Mom? Daddy?" she squeaked, and slid off the stool. "What are you doing here? You weren't supposed to be home until Friday."

Greta Benson dropped a striped straw handbag on the floor and reached for her daughter. Dana met her halfway and they embraced. Dana was much taller than her short, plump mother. Her height must have come from her father, who was nearly as tall as Kurt. Matthew wrapped his arms around his wife and daughter and the three swayed together. Kurt studied the wood framing the door.

Families were often a problem. Either they reinforced hysteria or encouraged denial or, worst of all, actively interfered in the case. Sometimes, though, they provided the rock of reason and support. As Kurt watched the three of them, he felt their closeness. A nice family with a lot of love and mutual caring.

Dana urged her parents into the family room and onto the couch. Kurt offered coffee. As Dana had told him, they were an elderly couple—in their seventies, he guessed. Dana's birth had probably been a hell of a surprise. Judging by the way they acted, he also figured she'd become the reason for their existence. Even seated, Greta kept her arm firmly around Dana's waist. Matthew with his stern face and rigid posture looked ready to fight to the death on his daughter's behalf.

"What are you doing here?" Dana clasped her mother's hand in both of hers. "You both look exhausted. What...?"

"You didn't tell us," Greta said, her voice shaky with accusation. "We had to learn it secondhand. The

Yarburoughs called to ask if there was anything they could do, and we didn't know what to tell them! We caught the first flight we could. Dana, what is happening?''

Dana lowered her face and her silky hair swung over her cheeks.

Kurt stepped in. "Dana didn't see any need to ruin your vacation with this situation."

"Situation," Matthew said gruffly. His eyes, paler blue, yet sharper than Dana's, snapped with angry light. "I fail to see how my daughter's arrest for murder qualifies as a mere situation, Mr. Saxon."

Kurt saw where Dana got her starch. No pussyfooting around with this white-haired gentleman. Kurt settled onto a club chair and leaned forward. He hung his clasped hands between his knees. "All right. The straight scoop, then. A man named Eddie Gordon was shot and killed. Witnesses claim Dana is the person who shot him. She was arrested on suspicion of murder. The police dropped the warrant for lack of evidence."

"It's mistaken identity," Dana said fervently. "I haven't hurt anyone. It's someone else, but she looks like me."

Matthew snaked an arm around his wife's shoulders.

Dana told them about the arrest and the videotape and the lineup, the strange woman who had called and how the woman looked a lot like her, but how she was left-handed and her widow's peak pointed the wrong way. She emphasized how Austin Tack had acquired the woman's license plate number, so now the police could start looking for her.

Greta regained her composure. Her large blue eyes were puzzled behind her thick glasses. She patted her husband's hand, then rose. "A mistake. I see. We were terribly worried. We tried to call, but all we got was your answering machine. We were so worried about you."

Dana winced. "I'm not answering the phone because of the reporters and crank callers. You should have left a message. You two look exhausted. Haven't you slept?"

Matthew had relaxed, somewhat. "Oh, you know us, princess, a catnap here and there. It's you we're worried about." Tension showed in his gnarled hands, now clenched tightly on his lap, and in the way he breathed through his mouth. He turned his attention on Kurt. "How serious is this, Mr. Saxon?"

"Call me Kurt. The police have eyewitnesses, but little else. It's serious, she could be arrested again, but I've got people working on it. I feel confident we can find the other woman."

"It's all so crazy, Daddy. You should see those detectives when they talk to me. You can just tell they think I'm lying. But we have proof the woman isn't me. She only looks like me."

In a small, almost whispered voice, Greta said, "Exactly like you?"

Dana covered her eyes with her hand. "It's incredible. I didn't believe it until I saw with my own eyes."

Kurt nodded. "We've got a good lead on her now. We'll find her."

"Oh, Mom, Daddy, I know I should have called, but there's really nothing you can do and I didn't want to ruin your vacation." Dana sighed. "Kurt and I are getting this straightened out. We have evidence the police have to believe." She stood, smiling tremulously. "I'll get some coffee. Unless you'd like something else?"

The telling look the Bensons exchanged made the back of Kurt's neck prickle. He didn't know them, so he couldn't interpret what it might mean, but he felt it. It was something about Matthew's clenched hands. The way both of them seemed to be avoiding Dana's eyes.

Greta plucked at her slacks.

Matthew swiped a hand over his mouth. "Perhaps we can help, Kurt," he said. "We may know who this other woman is."

Dana halted in midstride. "You know someone who looks like me?"

"Don't actually know her. Know of her."

Kurt jerked a pen from his shirt pocket and began patting other pockets. Dana fetched him a writing pad. "You've seen her on television?" he asked. "Work? Where have you seen her?"

"Oh, Matt," Greta murmured, and her eyes sparkled with tears. "We should have told her."

"Told her? Me? Told me what? You're scaring me. What's going on?"

Matthew rose slowly. He smoothed his hands over his wrinkled tropical print shirt. "You have a sister. An identical twin sister, to be exact."

Dana shook her head and her mouth stretched into an incredulous smile. "Pardon?"

"We couldn't take you both," Greta said. "We wanted to, but because of our age it was difficult enough, and besides, she had some problems and they didn't feel . . . they felt it was best."

"What are you talking about?"

Her father paced aimlessly around the room.

Whoa, Kurt thought. When Austin had pointed out the differences between Dana and the mystery woman, the first thing he'd thought of was an identical twin. He'd heard how twins often mirrored each other. One would be logical, the other creative; one right-handed, the other left-handed; their fingerprints were often reversed. Since Dana never mentioned the possibility—and shouldn't she know?—he'd figured it wasn't worthy of consideration.

"How could I have a twin sister and not know it?"

Greta looked helplessly at her husband. "You weren't quite four and very...hurt. You didn't talk for almost six months, and by then, you seemed to forget everything."

Matthew finally faced his daughter. "Your mom and I couldn't have kids of our own. We adopted you, princess."

She shook her head in vehement denial. "That's not true. Mom, I have your eyes. Everybody says so. And, Daddy, I'm tall like you and...and we both like to golf and play tennis . . . Why didn't you tell me?"

"The right time never—"

"The right time? I'm almost thirty years old. When did you figure I'd be adult enough to know? When I'm fifty?"

"You're our child," Matthew said. "We love you just as much as anyone could love a natural child. Adoptive, natural, it doesn't matter. We're still a family."

She stared blankly at her parents. "You never told me. I can't believe you never told me." She walked woodenly into the kitchen. She held a hand pressed to her side as if protecting something painfully tender.

Greta turned on the couch, watching her progress. "We never meant to hide anything from you. It wasn't a shameful secret. It just never came up. There was never a reason to talk about it. But now—"

"It never came up?" Mirthless laughter husked from her throat. "You couldn't have kids so you plucked me off the street and it never came up? All my life you told me to be honest, to tell the truth, and now I find out my whole life has been a lie? Oh, princess, you said, family is the most important thing in the world, but you never bothered to tell me I have a sister? How could you do this to me?"

Greta reached out both hands, her face twisted in a mute plea. "You're my baby."

"I don't even know who you are! I don't know who I am."

"Dana," Matthew said. "You've no call to speak to your mother that way. Now, sit down, we'll tell you what happened."

"You know, it's funny. I can understand Pauline. As much as it hurts, she's acting right in character.

Star Systems means everything to her, and if she has to knife me in the back to keep it, she'll do it. And Neal? What can I expect from him? He's always been selfish and self-centered. But you? I don't understand this at all.''

"Oh, princess," Greta said, "please, come sit down. Let us explain."

"My entire life is falling apart, I'm facing total ruination, and you come in here and knock my feet right out from under me."

Greta began to cry. Matthew was at her side in an instant.

Dana leaned on the kitchen counter, burying her face on her arm. Unable to stand it, Kurt went to her.

"Come on," he said quietly, and patted her back. "You're under a lot of stress, you've had a big shock, but you've got to be practical now."

Under her arm came a muffled "No, I don't."

"I know we should have told you." Matthew fetched his wife's purse.

Greta fished tissues out of her purse and wiped her eyes. "You are not a shameful secret. It just never came up. You're our daughter in every way except blood. No one will ever be able to tell me you're not my baby."

Dana lifted her head. Tears shimmered, poised to fall. Kurt urged her to return to the family room and seated her on the club chair. Assuming his most lawyerly expression, he stood so he could see all three faces. He'd never dealt with anything like this, and for one of the few times in his life, he felt completely at a loss for what to do or say.

"Under ideal circumstances," he said, "the three of you could talk this out. We don't have the luxury right now. The police will be here soon. Mr. and Mrs. Benson, I need you to answer some questions."

"We'll do anything to help our daughter." Matthew colored the word daughter with feeling.

"Do the adoption papers mention the twin sister?"

"No," Matthew answered.

"Tell me about the adoption." He prepared to take notes.

"Dana and her sister are identical twins. Peas in a pod. We wanted to adopt both, but the orphanage director wouldn't allow it. The girls had been abandoned, and no one knew anything about their history or where they came from. Dana was a sweet child, but she didn't speak. The people at the orphanage thought she might be retarded. But we knew she wasn't. She was wounded somehow, that's all."

"And her sister?"

"A little animal. Wild and afraid of everybody and very destructive. Everyone feared she'd end up in a mental institution and so refused to consider her for adoption. We took Dana home. At first she wouldn't speak and she had night terrors. Night after night. Afraid of the dark, animals, strangers. Many was the night Greta sat up with her, rocking her."

"The fears faded away." Greta beseeched Dana with her eyes. "You began to talk. You always did well in school." Her lips trembled in a hopeful smile. "Didn't you, dear? Honor society, straight A's."

"Dana, you've never remembered the twin?"

She looked between Kurt and her parents. In her eyes he found confusion, suspicion and hurt. "I don't remember anything. I'm not quite sure I'm buying this."

"I've no call to lie," Matthew said stiffly.

"You've lied to me all my life. Why not now?"

Greta began to cry again. Her husband patted her back and murmured soothingly. Dana's expression crumpled and she flopped back on the chair, with her arms crossed tightly, chin trembling and eyes glazed.

"Greta and I often wondered what became of her parents. They were pretty little girls, hair like white silk and those big blue eyes. Can't imagine anyone just throwing them away."

"When she seemed to forget," Greta said, "it was a blessing." She tightened her grip on her husband's hand. "No more nightmares, no more phobias. She was so young, it seemed natural for her to forget. That's why we didn't tell you, princess. You forgot and then you were such a happy child. We didn't want to dredge up old horrors."

It made sense to Kurt. The slight easing in Dana's tension told him it made some sense to her, too. He asked, "So you don't know what happened to the other twin?"

"No. I'm not certain the orphanage still exists, either."

"There'll be records somewhere. I'll need a statement from both of you along with her adoption records."

Matthew gave his wife a final pat and rose. Hands behind his back, he paced the room. For a moment his gaze lingered on Kurt's dumbbells.

"Despite my daughter's innocence, defending her will be an expensive proposition."

"It can be, yes, sir," Kurt answered. He liked this old man who appeared tough as Texas itself.

"My wife and I will never appear on 'Lifestyles of the Rich and Famous,' but we're well settled. I own Benson Realty, have for nigh on thirty-five years. I'm semiretired, but the business is still healthy. I also own more than a hundred rental properties in the city. Spare no expense, Kurt. I want my daughter cleared."

"I can pay my own bills, Daddy," Dana said.

Matthew exchanged a meaningful look with Kurt. "Always cash poor. Staying in fashion is more important than having a savings account. Have your office send all the bills to me."

"Daddy—"

"It's settled. Princess, you should move back home where your mother and I can take care of you. Has the media been a problem?"

"I'm staying right here, Daddy. I need to stay here. There are . . . complications." She pushed out of the chair. "I don't want to drag you into it." She returned to the kitchen.

Greta followed her daughter. The women huddled head-to-head, Greta speaking in a low earnest tone and Dana staring at the floor, a rebellious expression on her face.

"What sort of complications?" Matthew demanded to know. He peered closely at Kurt's face as if suspecting the bruises were involved.

Kurt needed this man. He had the funds to pay for a top-notch defense and the willingness to do so. Whether Dana wanted it or not, he also offered the support she so desperately needed. Yet Kurt understood Dana's reluctance to involve her parents fully in the case. Despite her hurt and confusion, she wanted to protect them.

Greater good, he told himself. He urged Matthew to follow him into the once-formal dining room where they could speak privately. Kurt closed the double doors.

Matthew looked around at Kurt's impromptu office. "You've moved in."

"Yes, sir. If you'll have a seat, I'll explain why."

Matthew took the news of Dragon-man and Carl Perriman much as Kurt expected. The man remained calm and in control of his emotions. His only comment was, "You can assure me, then, you and this private eye friend of yours are qualified to protect my daughter."

"I got sloppy once." He fingered the bandage on his forehead. "It won't happen again."

"Do you think this Dragon-man is still a danger to Dana?"

"Yes."

"Why aren't the police protecting her?"

"I can do it better."

Matthew puffed his cheeks and made noises with his tongue. He fingered papers on the tabletop. "What do you wish us to do?"

The question was music to Kurt's ears. He could trust this man to do the right things. "I would like you and your wife to go home. I'll need you to tell the police about the adoption, but before you do, I'll send one of my people to take your statements." He began writing out a list. "We'll need Dana's adoption papers, the name of the orphanage, the names of anyone you can remember who was involved. Lawyers, judges, social workers.''

''I understand.'' Matthew accepted Kurt's list. He folded it neatly and placed it in his shirt pocket.

''If your friends or acquaintances ask you about the case, please do not discuss it. Remember, anything anyone says can be used in a court of law. Do you have an attorney?''

''Robert Quintana.''

''I know him. Good man. If you have any questions or concerns about my methods, feel free to contact him. Won't hurt my heart. Any questions?''

''Only one. What are your qualifications?''

Kurt grinned. ''Twelve years as a criminal defense attorney. I'm not high profile, I'm not rich. I work hard. I care about your daughter and what happens to her.'' He gave Matthew a business card.

The old man studied the card carefully. ''I will ask my attorney about you. We'll see what he says.''

Chapter Thirteen

After her parents had left, Dana went upstairs to her bedroom. She closed the door and stood with her hands flat against the wood. Breathing deeply, drawing air to the very base of her lungs, she sought answers to the formless questions swirling through her mind. She felt as if some greater force were shredding her life piece by piece, rebuilding her into something new and alien, something nameless and alone.

The cheval glass drew her. She stared at her reflection. The face was the same as it had been this morning when she awakened. She tested her tongue against her teeth. She fingered her biceps and the base of her throat. She looked the same, she felt the same, but who was she?

Kurt knocked on the door.

"Not now," she called. "Go away."

He entered the room, anyway.

With a heavy sigh, she faced him. "You don't listen very well."

"I listen fine, it's the paying attention part I usually ignore. You don't need to be alone."

"I don't need you to tell me what I need. Or what I think or how I should feel or even what I should do. Get out."

He sat on the edge of her bed and leaned forward with his elbows on his knees. At the window, she looked out at the cul-de-sac. One of her neighbors was weeding a flowerbed in her front yard. Her two pre-schoolers were playing with a soccer ball. Dana envied the woman her quiet, normal life and the security of her young family.

"The cops will be here any time now."

"I don't want to tell them about my sister."

"We don't have a choice. It's you or her, babe. Since she's the shooter, I vote for her."

"It was self-defense. Eddie Gordon tried to kill her and she fought back." She looked over her shoulder at him. "And you know it."

"Sure I know it. I also know the cops won't drop it. That means an arrest and a trial. It means in the next few months, or years even, you'll become an expert on the legal system. Knowledge I'm a hundred percent certain you'd rather not have. You'll spend hundreds of thousands of dollars on your defense. One way or another you'll lose Star Systems. The videotape will eventually be released to the public, and television stations will have a field day grinding your name into the mud. Once that happens it won't matter if you're acquitted. The public will always believe you were guilty and only got off because of a technicality. Some writer will put together a quickie true-crime book about the golden girl gone bad. Is that what you want?"

She swiped at her burning eyes. "You know it isn't."

"Then we tell the cops about your sister. It's the only way."

A lump formed in her throat. All her life she'd longed for brothers and sisters. Since her parents were both only children, she didn't even have the consolation of cousins. How she'd envied children who belonged to large families. The noise, the laughter, the sense of belonging and having someone to share toys and dreams with.

Now out of the blue, in the most unexpected way possible, she had a sister. And in the same stroke of fate, she was about to lose her again.

"Why can't I remember her, Kurt? Shouldn't I feel something? Some...sense of her out there?"

He came to stand behind her. He rested his hands on her shoulders and his cheek against her hair.

"A few days ago I thought I knew everything. Who I was, what I wanted. Part of me is so damned angry. Mom and Daddy were my world, and all of a sudden, it's all a lie. I don't know who I am or where I came from. They kept from me something I wanted with all my heart."

"They thought they were doing the right thing. They wanted to adopt her, too, but they couldn't. They didn't split you apart, the system did."

"I know. I honestly know that." She leaned against him, drawing on his steadiness. His warm breath caressed her cheek. "I'm so confused." Pain rippled through her and she shuddered, closing her eyes.

Kurt crossed his arms in front of her, cupping her elbows. He rocked her gently back and forth.

"I feel as if I'm losing everything. My business, my friends, my reputation, and now my identity. There has to be a reason for all this. Some meaning or purpose."

"They're here."

She opened her eyes. A tan Chevy had stopped in front of her house. Callister and Tannenbaum got out and squinted into the sunshine. The sun competed fiercely with scattered clouds now joining forces over the city. Callister pointed at the southern sky and said something that caused Tannenbaum to shake his head.

Dana's belly knotted.

"I want to find her first, Kurt. I want to know what happened."

"What if she has mental problems? What if she sought you out to do you harm? She was carrying a gun."

Was her twin, as her parents had hinted, insane? Was she evil, wicked, a psychopath? Where had she been for the past twenty-five years? In a mental institution or prison? Or had she been adopted, too? Did she have a family who loved her, or had she been lost in the faceless system, shuttled from home to home, loved by no one with no one to call her own?

She touched her face, fingering the smooth skin she'd always taken such pains to pamper. All her life she'd been acknowledged as pretty. A few thought of her as beautiful. Did her sister think she was beautiful? Was she married? Did she have children? A thousand questions tumbled through her mind, and with them came a burning desire to know the answers.

She watched the detectives follow the curved concrete path leading to her front door. "They'll do the same thing to her they're doing to me. But we know she isn't guilty."

Kurt made a soft cynical noise. "She asked to meet you in a seedy bar and she had a gun. Sister or no sister, there's a good chance she wasn't looking for a friendly reunion. We have to assume the worst, Dana. Let the cops figure out the self-defense angle."

"She's my sister." *Sister* tasted so odd in her mouth. Why couldn't she remember? "I don't want to assume the worst. I want to find her. Please, I know you think I'm crazy, but no matter what she's done, she's still my sister."

"Dana—"

"I'm not suggesting anything illegal. You should know me better than that by now. I'd never dream of harboring a fugitive or helping her escape justice. I just want to talk to her, I want to know what she wants. I need to know."

"She looked you up. There's a reason for it."

Dana nodded. "Exactly. I want, *need* to know that reason. Please, this one thing. Once we find her, I'll do whatever you advise. All I ask is that we find her first."

"I can't make that promise."

The doorbell rang. The soft chimes made icy, prickly fingers creep up her back. She shivered and turned in his arms. "Please. Let's give Austin a few more days to find her."

His pale eyes went cold and hard. "Damn it, don't look at me like that." He stared over her head.

"You have all those brothers and sisters. You love them, right? You'd do anything for them. I know you would because that's how you are. If one of them were in trouble, you'd move heaven and earth to help."

He wrenched away from her hands. Chest heaving, he planted his fists on his hips. "You fight dirty."

Something broke loose in her heart and flooded her with warmth. "Daddy always said I was a born salesperson."

"Twenty-four hours," he forced out reluctantly. "It'll give me time to do some research into the adoption. But that's it."

Reason said it was the best she could hope for. "Thank you."

"I must be crazy to get this involved with a client."

"You started it." She smiled.

"I sure did." He took her hand. He gave her a quick, heartfelt kiss before they went downstairs to face the police.

Being interviewed in her home was different from being interviewed at the police station. Callister took Kurt into the dining room; Tannenbaum talked to Dana in the family room.

Detective Tannenbaum was mild, smiling and soft-spoken. He graciously accepted a glass of iced tea; he admired her medieval figurines and asked about the history of her nineteenth-century bird's-eye maple secretary; he invited her to call him Al.

They talked about Carl and Dragon-man, Pauline and her relationship with Neal. She told him how Jilly had found her office unlocked on Wednesday morning, which meant Eddie Gordon may have broken in to look for the pictures which didn't arrive until Thursday. She expressed puzzlement along with the detective about why Dragon-man wanted the pictures.

Dana liked him and admired his listening skills. He'd make a good salesman.

Callister finished with Kurt. When the two men joined her and Tannenbaum, she noticed the detective looked as grim and hostile as before. Kurt's face was carefully blank.

"How you doing, Al?" Callister asked.

"Dana is being very cooperative. This is a real interesting story." He thanked her for the iced tea.

The detectives departed, carrying a copy of the photographs and Dragon-man's gun.

Drained, Dana sank to a chair and rested her chin on a fist. "Thank goodness we're finally getting somewhere. Do you think they'll find Dragon-man—"

"They aren't biting," Kurt interrupted.

"What?"

"They don't believe a word."

"Maybe Callister is being stubborn, but Al was completely—"

"Sweet, kind and credulous. Yeah, yeah, I know how he operates. Face it, the story sounds idiotic. They're probably looking at the pictures and laughing their heads off. Pauline is going to end up on every bulletin board in the station."

"But Al said he'd go through mug shots and see if he can find men who resemble Dragon-man."

"Even if he does, he won't find him. I have a feeling he's from Louisiana or Mississippi. He's definitely out of state. Odds are, he's been in prison, but not around here. How much digging are they going to do for a guy they think we invented?"

"But Carl's apartment, the blood..."

"I imagine the cops looked over the place and talked to neighbors. I bet nobody saw anything, nobody heard anything. For all the cops know, Carl's a crappy housekeeper. Or he's on vacation and we trashed the place to back up our story."

"What about the gun?"

"It's cheap and filthy, like we fished it out of a ditch. They might get lucky and trace it, but I doubt it very much. Goofs like Dragon-man aren't real conscientious about registering firearms."

He passed a hand over his eyes, and his big shoulders slumped. "I didn't help matters by telling the doctor I tripped and hit my head on a door." He cursed violently and leapt to his feet. "Ah, hell, it doesn't matter. They don't believe us, but who cares?"

"Did we accomplish anything? Anything good, that is?"

"I doubt it. Let's hope we didn't do you any harm."

KURT BURST INTO DANA'S bedroom. Fresh from the shower, garbed in a towel, she clutched her terry-cloth robe and screamed at him to get out. She grabbed a bottle of perfume off the dresser and prepared to throw it.

"We found her!" He thrust a fist of victory into the air.

She lowered her throwing arm. "My sister?"

"I just got off the phone with Austin. He ran down the license plate and came up with the name Star Jones."

"What kind of name is that?" A funny feeling tickled her as she remembered when she and Pauline had started the business. For days they'd argued over a name. They'd wanted something classy, simple to remember, high-tech. From nowhere Dana had come up with Star Systems.

Maybe she did remember her sister, after all.

Her knees wobbled and she clung to the dresser for support. Kurt was at her side in an instant.

"Are you all right?"

She nodded dumbly. Her sister had a name. "Where is she?"

"The address is in Wichita Falls. Austin is on his way now to see what he can find."

"I want to go."

"We've got things to do here. Don't worry, Austin will let us know as soon as he finds anything. Are you sure you're all right?"

She groped behind her for the bed and sat down. "What will he do if he finds her?"

"Talk to her."

He sat and the mattress sagged under his weight. Dana compensated for the shift, and the towel gaped over her thighs. Aware of Kurt finding the display of interest, she crossed her legs. That made things worse.

No, what made it worse was liking the way he looked at her. Heightened awareness seemed to make the air crackle. Her emotions jumbled in a tangle of fear, gratitude, excitement and apprehension.

She could smell him. His hair was damp from his shower and the scent of shampoo wafted to her nose, along with the spicy warmth of after-shave. She told herself to jump up, throw him out and get dressed.

"We're going to talk to Patty today."

Distracted by his nearness, she drew a blank.

"The bartender at O'Dooley's who may have witnessed the shooting."

"Oh. Has she agreed to talk to us?"

"Haven't asked, but her shift starts at two o'clock." He tapped his fingers against his knees. "Sometimes, if we catch witnesses at work, they talk just to get rid of us."

"I see." Her throat felt thick. She watched his hands. Sunlight through the windows made the hairs glint with golden light. His fingers were long and muscular, the nails blunt. Imagining those hands having free rein on her body turned her weak inside.

She wanted him. She wanted to kiss him and watch his eyes turn from glittering ice to heated smoke. She wanted to explore the fascinating array of sinuous muscle in his back and bury her nose in his hair and test his long legs against hers. She wanted to see if his skin tasted as good as it smelled.

Wanting made her dizzy.

"Guess I ought to get out of here." His voice had lowered to a rumble.

"I'll be dressed in a few minutes." She stared fiercely at the fireplace. If she looked at him ... if she read desire in the curve of his smile or the gleam in his eyes ...

"Dana?"

"Yes?"

"We have a lot to do."

She wanted to squirm against the liquid heat melting her inner thighs. "We had better get going."

"Guess we better." He walked quickly to the door.

Disappointment tattered her insides. Where was the ravishment he promised? As soon as she thought it, she chided herself for being an idiot. She had made her wishes perfectly clear and so had he.

He opened the door. "By the way," he said. "You have the most incredible neck and shoulders I've ever seen in my life."

A frisson left her tingling.

He closed the door behind him.

"You do want an affair, casual or otherwise," she mumbled, disgusted with herself. But not quite disgusted enough to stop imagining what kind of lover Kurt Saxon might be. If he lived up to his kisses, he'd kill her with sheer pleasure.

"ARE YOU SURE I SHOULD go in there?" Dana asked.

O'Dooley's Bar and Grill wasn't as terrible looking as Dana had imagined, although it had no windows and a dirt parking lot. It was housed in a flat-roofed building, flanked by a laundromat on one side and an empty storefront on the other.

She couldn't imagine why Star had wanted to meet her in a place like this.

"I don't want to leave you out here alone," Kurt said.

"What if somebody recognizes me?" She wore sunglasses, and Kurt had given her a baseball cap. She didn't like it. It had a beer company logo embroidered on the front and the bill was sweat-stained. It made her head itch. Besides, it looked ridiculous with her peach-colored blouse, tan jacket and slacks.

Kurt snickered and flipped up the sun visor on the passenger side. "Quit staring at yourself in the mirror. You look fine."

"I look stupid."

"Let's go."

She tugged the cap lower on her face and accompanied him into the bar.

Except for a woman behind the bar, the place was deserted. Talk, laughter and the sound of rattling glass came from the back room. Booths lined one wall. Television sets were mounted in every corner. The television closest to the bar played a soap opera.

Kurt sat on a stool at the bar. Dana did the same.

The bartender was a young woman of average height. She wore a great deal of makeup, and her brown hair frizzed away from her face in impressive wings. She greeted them with a smile.

Kurt ordered two beers. When the woman placed the glasses in front of them, Kurt asked, "Are you Patty Cartwell?"

She gave him a come-hither grin. "Who wants to know?"

Kurt gave her a business card. She read it and the smile turned into a frown. "A lawyer. What's this all about?"

"The shooting of Eddie Gordon."

Patty recoiled as if they had communicable diseases. "I didn't see nothing. I told the cops already. I don't have nothing to do with it."

"Patty," Kurt said, "I'm not working for the police or the prosecutor's office." He curled both hands around his beer glass. "The way I hear it, you were in the parking lot when the shooting occurred."

She slapped a rag against the bar. "Shoot! It's that private eye, isn't it? Coming in here with his cute smile and tight butt, talking to all the girls. I told them to keep my name out of it." She shook her head so violently her hair flopped. "I can't talk to you."

"You talked to your friends about it. I know it's eating at you. You have a story to tell."

"I can't." She turned away, fussing with liquor bottles.

"It's Bob. You don't want to involve him."

"Leave him out of this. We didn't do nothing wrong. The cops got all kinds of witnesses. They know who killed that guy so they don't need me." Her mouth pulled into a weak, pleading smile. "You don't understand about me and Bobby. See, he's married, but it ain't a real marriage. She won't let him touch her or nothing. His wife is crazy, that's why he can't divorce her. She's in therapy and all."

Dana's stomach turned. This deluded young woman probably loved good old Bobby with all her heart.

"I understand," Kurt said. "But I need you to understand. My client has been falsely accused of a crime she hasn't committed. This is Dana Benson." He laid a hand on Dana's shoulder. "She wasn't here."

Patty's eyes widened. "Oh, gawd," she breathed.

"This is the first time I've ever been inside this bar," Dana said.

"Everybody saw you."

"They saw a woman who looks like me."

"And we have reason to believe the shooting was in self-defense." Kurt nodded.

Patty lifted a shoulder. "Well, sure, it was self-defense. The cops gotta know that." She peered suspiciously at Dana. "It wasn't you? I saw your picture and everything. Everyone says it's you."

"Why do you say it was self-defense?"

"I can't...if Bobby..."

"We don't have to involve Bobby. He never has to know you talked to us. What did you see, Patty? Why is it self-defense?"

She threw down her rag. "I read that story in the paper saying it was murder. I told Bobby he has to tell the police, but he won't. He says if I drag him into it, we're through. I can't lose him! He's my whole world."

Kurt drank some beer. He wiped his mouth with the back of his hand. "Listen to me very carefully, Patty. If my client is arrested and charged, the case will go to trial. I will have no choice except to subpoena you and Bobby to testify."

"We'll say we didn't see nothing."

"I'll put you on the stand, under oath. If you lie, it'll be perjury and you'll go to jail. Now, I know you've talked to some of your friends about the shooting. I'll subpoena them, too. How is Bobby going to explain that to his wife?"

Her eyes shimmered. "You can't do that."

Dana felt sorry for her. She stared at her beer.

"I will if I have to."

"If I tell you what I saw, will you promise not to make me go to court? Will you keep Bobby out of it?"

Dana looked at Patty and held her breath.

"I can't promise, but if you don't talk to me, I guarantee you and Bobby will end up in court. So tell me what you saw."

Patty surprised Dana with a smile. "Your mouthpiece is a real mean guy. Plays hardball."

"I know," Dana agreed. "Please help us, Ms. Cartwell. We don't want to cause trouble for you, honestly."

"All right, all right." She closed her eyes. "Gawd, Bobby's gonna kill me. What do you want to know?"

Kurt brought out his pen and notebook. "Tell me what you saw."

"I was on break." She pointed. "Bobby and I were in his car down at the end of the parking lot. The light's out, so it's private. We weren't doing nothing, just talking. Kissing a little. You know. Then Bobby, he says, better get down, looks like a fight. So I look and there's three guys. Oh, I guess it was two guys and a girl." She looked at Dana. "It wasn't you?"

"Are you sure there were three people?" Kurt asked. "Can you describe them?"

"Not really. It was dark. They was over by the fence where some cars were parked. Like I said, the light's burnt out."

"But you are positive there were three?"

"Definitely. One had hold of the girl." She grabbed her upper arm to demonstrate. "Jerking her around."

"How close were you to them?"

"Bobby was parked at the end of the row, and they was across the driveway. What's that, maybe twenty feet? So anyways, I tell Bobby, don't look like a fight, looks like they're robbing the guy. I thought it was a guy. I didn't know it was a girl until later."

"Did you hear them say anything? Screams?"

"It was kind of cold that night. We had the windows up and we was playing my Billy Ray Cyrus tape. I didn't hear nothing. Just saw a lot of pushing and pulling."

"Then what happened?"

"The three of them kind of stumbled. You know, went down in a heap. Like football players. I don't know who was on the top or bottom. All of a sudden one takes off running. Had to be the girl, 'cause she's running back toward here. That's when we heard the shot."

Kurt's forehead furrowed in a deep frown. "You're positive about that?"

"I think so." She nodded. "Yeah, I'm sure. 'Cause then Bobby grabs my head and pushes me down. Him and me, we're whispering, all scared and everything. We knew it was a gun right off. Bobby's got lots of guns. He knows what they sound like. I do, too. Then we don't hear nothing and Bobby kind of peeks and looks around. He's saying, oh, hell, a guy got shot, he's lying on the ground, and then people come running to see. We're scootched down on the seat, hiding. People are yelling and stuff. So Bobby and me sneak out of the car and everybody's looking at the dead guy so nobody sees us." She pointed again. "Bobby went across the street to the Taco Bell, and I came back here. He came back after the cops left and got his car."

Kurt studied what he'd written. "The police aren't aware there were three people involved."

"I told you everything. I don't want to talk to them. They'll make me tell about Bobby, and he'll get in trouble. He's gonna be real mad if he finds out I talked to you."

"The police don't know it's self-defense. They can't know. No one else saw the shooting. No one else saw the third man." He brought out another business card, flipped it over and wrote on the back. "This is the name and number of the detective in charge of the case. Trust me, he's not interested in getting you or Bobby in trouble." He slid the card across the shiny bar top. "All he wants is the truth."

Patty crossed her arms, tucking her hands under her armpits. She stared unhappily at the card. "I'll think about it."

Kurt swiveled on the stool and stood. He brought out his wallet and threw a ten-dollar bill on the bar. "Think about this thing going to trial, and subpoenas, and Bobby's wife sitting in the gallery listening to him testify. Come on, Dana."

Chapter Fourteen

"Do you think Patty will talk to the police?" Dana asked. She and Kurt sat in a coffee shop about a block from O'Dooley's. Dana had removed the ridiculous cap but kept wearing the sunglasses. She stirred creamer into her coffee.

"I don't know if we want her to." He flipped through his notebook.

"How can you say that? The other man had to have been Dragon-man."

"Star was running before she shot Gordon. That means she got away, then fired."

"Dragon-man had a gun. Gordon probably did, too. It's still self-defense."

"She didn't scream, she didn't yell for help. She might say she fired to keep them from chasing her, but convincing the cops of that will be tough. The best she may be able to hope for will be negligent homicide. This isn't looking good."

"If they catch Dragon-man—"

"If, Dana, *if*. I'm not certain anyone is looking for him."

Her buoyant mood burst like a bubble. "Is she going to prison?"

"Her fleeing the scene doesn't look good. We'll go for self-defense, but a lot will depend on her. It depends on if she has an arrest record. I want to know why she had a gun in the first place. Why she ran. Why she hasn't come forward." He gestured at her with a spoon. "Chances are she saw the articles in the newspaper. Saw your name, knows you're taking the rap. More and more, it's looking like she wanted something besides a happy reunion."

Dana tried to remember the telephone conversation with Star. At the time, though, she'd been concentrating on a proposal to win the Wainwright account and the call had interrupted her. Star's caginess had annoyed her, so she hadn't paid much attention. She couldn't recall a single word.

A soft beep came from Kurt's pager. He unhooked it from his belt and eyed the readout. "It's Austin, calling long-distance. He may have found her." He left to find a pay telephone.

Dana couldn't decide if finding Star was good news or bad news. She fidgeted, watching the few customers and the orange-and-white-clad waitresses.

Kurt was gone twenty minutes. He looked pleased when he returned. She signaled the waitress to bring them fresh coffee.

"Austin is in Wichita Falls. Star Jones does live there. She's employed by an arts and crafts co-op as a courier." He looked down at his notes. "Her description is, five feet nine inches tall, slim, about one hundred and thirty pounds, very light blond air and blue eyes.''

''You just described me.''

''It's definitely her.'' Austin showed your picture to neighbors and to people at the co-op. They all thought it was Star.''

''So she's gainfully employed. That's good. Right?''

''It is. Also good is that she was in Dallas on legitimate business. She transports paintings, pottery, jewelry, artsy crap. Dallas is part of her regular delivery run. And get this, she has a permit to carry a concealed weapon.''

Dana sat back against the vinyl booth. ''That means her carrying a gun has nothing to do with me.''

''That's right. But there's more.''

Dana rubbed the base of her throat. Her heart thudded heavily.

''She returned to Wichita Falls on Wednesday. According to her boss, she showed up on time and didn't mention anything unusual had happened.''

Dana's mouth dropped open.

Kurt nodded in derision. ''According to him, she was acting perfectly normal. He has no idea she ran into any kind of trouble at all. On the day you were arrested, she left town on another run.''

''Where?''

''Austin can't find out. Apparently, she transports items that are pretty valuable. Sometimes she carries large amounts of cash. Her schedule is top secret.'' He held up a finger. ''However, we do know Star doesn't have a criminal record. She's bonded, and that means the company ran a security check on her. A license to carry a concealed weapon means she doesn't have a history of mental disease. At least, she's never been in an institution.''

"What if she doesn't know she killed Gordon?" Dana reached across the table and tapped his notebook. "She carries a weapon. She must be on the alert for robberies. Gordon and Dragon-man are fighting with her. She thinks it's a robbery. She gets away and fires the gun, as a warning, but doesn't know she hit anybody. It's dark, she can't see.''

"It's possible, but we'll have a hell of a time convincing the police. She knows better than to leave the scene of a shooting.''

"We need Dragon-man or Carl," she muttered, and opened her purse. She brought out the packet of pictures. She found the picture of Pauline and Neal locked in a passionate embrace. How tasteless, she thought, making out in a public place. Anyone could have seen them.

She fanned the pictures across the tabletop. "This is crazy. No wonder the police think we're lying. Even if Pauline knew Carl took these pictures, she wouldn't care. I've known her for years. Nothing embarrasses her. As far as her love life is concerned, she's utterly shameless.''

"What about Neal? It might be worthwhile for him to keep you from knowing about him and Pauline.''

No matter how hard she tried, she couldn't reconcile a man who had a conniption fit if his tie wasn't tied correctly with hiring a character like Dragon-man.

"He's hoping to make partner in the firm. What happens if his bosses find out he's involved in a love triangle with two of his clients?"

"You make it sound sordid and ugly. I never even slept with him."

Kurt's eyebrows lifted. "You didn't?"

She covered her eyes with a hand and laughed. "No, I didn't, and it's none of your business." She picked up a picture of Neal and Pauline walking hand in hand. "Even if I had, all they have to say is these were taken after we broke up. I didn't fire Neal after we stopped seeing each other. Why would he think I'd fire him over this?"

She noticed something else in the pictures. Sorting through the prints, she found eight of the twenty-four showed other people. "Kurt?" She turned a photo around and indicated the people in the background. "What if it doesn't have anything to do with Pauline and Neal at all? Maybe there was somebody else in the park that day."

He studied the pictures intently. All the people were at a distance, their features indistinct. As for what they were doing, there was no telling.

Finally, he said, "Three men. Oh, ho, Carl might have inadvertently witnessed a drug deal. We may have something big here."

"Even if those men saw Carl, how would they know it was him?"

"Only Carl can answer that. You have no idea where he might be hiding out?"

"I've called everyone who knows him. Nobody has seen him or talked to him in weeks. At least, no one will admit it.'' She gathered the pictures into a neat stack. "I know who knows where and when these pictures were taken. Pauline and Neal.''

"You're willing to confront them?''

She slipped the pictures into the packet. "I keep hearing Pauline say, 'the guy you shot.' Even if I had shot Gordon, I'd expect her to support me. But she doesn't care. This thing with Neal proves it." She sighed and shook her head.

"This hurts you," Kurt said quietly.

"I've worked so hard for Star Systems. It's one of those brilliantly simple ideas that worked. For years I lived hand to mouth, scrimping and saving, putting everything I had into the company, going into debt. But it's always been more than the money. It was winning the accounts, pitting myself against the competition. It was making it in spite of the odds. Do you know what I mean?''

"You like the challenge.''

"And it hasn't been easy. Those good-old-boy networks are firmly entrenched. We've had to overcome our share of prejudices. Sometimes it's discouraging. I'd go for weeks without a sale, or equipment would break down, or we'd mess up somehow. Through it all, there was always Pauline. She'd encourage me, I'd encourage her. I always thought she was my best friend. I truly did.''

"What are you going to do?''

"I honestly do not know. The only thing I know for certain is my partnership with her is over.''

DANA FELT LIKE A STRANGER in Star Systems. The place even seemed to smell different. She didn't recognize the middle-aged woman sitting behind Jilly's desk.

"May I help you?" the woman asked. She gave Kurt an uncertain look.

"I'm Dana Benson. Who are you?"

The woman whipped her head around to look at the nameplate on Dana's office door. "Oh, Miss Benson, sorry, I'm Liz Sanders from the temp agency."

"I see. Is Pauline Kidder in?" She headed for Pauline's office.

"Miss Kidder is—" she leafed through a stack of papers "—at Chusak Electronics. She said she probably won't be back in today."

Chusak was one of Star Systems's largest accounts. The only reason she could think of for Pauline to go there was that they had threatened to pull their data. Terrific.

"Where's Jilly?"

Liz looked blank.

"The secretary you're subbing for?"

"I don't know. I was just—"

"Never mind. If Pauline does come in later, tell her—"

"Dana!" Alison Torres swept into the reception area. Her dark eyes flashed. Dana had never seen the programmer so excited.

"Thank the stars for a voice of reason!" Alison exclaimed. "I'm so glad you're back."

"I'm not really back, I'm just looking for Pauline. Is everything all right?"

Alison snorted, looking daggers at the temporary secretary. "You don't know? It figures."

"Know what?"

Alison indicated Dana's office. She cupped a hand around her ear as if to say, watch out for unwanted listeners.

Once in her office, Dana introduced Kurt to Alison, explaining, "Alison is a programmer. She works in data storage. So what's up, Alison? Why do you need a voice of reason?"

"Because Pauline has lost her ever-lovin' mind. She fired Jilly and Sue."

Dana had to sit down. "You've got to be kidding."

Alison perched on a corner of the desk and picked up a letter opener. "Wish I was kidding, but I'm not. Pauline went loco yesterday. She says Jilly was stealing confidential data. Didn't even give her notice. She called security and had them watch Jilly clean out her desk then escort her from the building."

Dana rubbed her aching temples. "So why did she fire Sue?"

"Who is Sue?" Kurt asked.

"She's the bookkeeper who replaced Carl. Well?"

"It had something to do with Jilly. I don't know what, but Pauline went off on her, too. Boom, got rid of both of them. Said they were in cahoots, conspiring against her and stealing Star Systems blind. You know it's all a damned lie. Then this morning, Chusak called wanting to close out their account. They said their legal department recommended it." Alison waggled her thick eyebrows. "I guess they're dumb enough to believe what they read in the paper. Pauline went ballistic. She's over there now, but I'm telling you, the state she's in, she's going to make it worse. She was talking about lawsuits for breach of contract.''

''Good heavens.''

''She may be a wizard with machines, but she don't know jack about customer relations. We need you back, Dana. I know you're having problems, but this is serious.''

''You don't know how serious,'' Dana muttered. It sounded as if she didn't have to do anything about dissolving her partnership—Pauline was going to bankrupt the company all by herself. ''What exactly was Jilly supposed to have been stealing?''

''She wasn't stealing anything. All she had were account books and some invoices. She was probably going to help Sue catch up on the tax paperwork, but Pauline never gave her a chance to explain. She wouldn't listen.''

Knowledge hit her like a blow to the solar plexus. Dana spun around on the chair. ''Jilly!'' she exclaimed to Kurt. ''I am so stupid.''

Kurt cocked his head. ''What is it?''

''It's Jilly. For the past few weeks she's been acting strange. Edgy and nervous, acting guilty. Pauline has been on her back constantly.'' She smacked her head with the heel of her hand. ''Why didn't I realize it? Carl and Jilly were always close. She's been helping him find evidence.''

''And she knows where he is,'' Kurt said with a smile.

''I'd bet money on it.''

"What are you talking about?" Alison asked. "Evidence? Carl? Does this have to do with the police thing?"

"We don't know yet." Dana grabbed her purse. "I've got to go. If by chance Pauline does return today, don't bother telling her I was here. I'll talk to her when I'm good and ready."

As they hurried downstairs to the garage, Kurt said, "Why wouldn't Jilly come to you about Carl?"

"Why should she? I fired Carl. I believed Pauline over him. He sends me pictures, and Dragon-man beats him up. He must be scared to death imagining Pauline and I are trying to kill him. When Jilly found my office unlocked, she almost panicked. Looking back, she must have known it was Dragon-man. Why are you looking at me like that?"

He had his head cocked, and his smile was crooked. The corners of his eyes crinkled in amusement. "Indignation sits well with you."

"Why shouldn't I be indignant?" She poked his solid chest with a finger. "You're right, I'm too trusting. I accept too much at face value. Pauline has lied to me and stabbed me in the back. She fired the best secretary I ever had. I have had it with her."

Despite heavy traffic, they made it across the city to Jilly's apartment building in record time. In her eagerness to find Carl, Dana didn't even mind Kurt's road-racer driving style.

Halfway up the stairs to the second-floor apartment, Dana asked, "What do we say to her? How do we convince her I'm on Carl's side?"

"Tell the truth. Be straight. That always works best for me."

She found his hand and grasped it. He squeezed her fingers in return. At Jilly's door, she knocked.

Jilly's roommate answered. The brunette, who had always reminded Dana of a young Joan Collins, was eating from a quart-sized carton of yogurt. "Well, hi, Dana," Marci said. "What are you doing here?"

"Is Jilly in?"

Marci smiled around a spoonful of yogurt at Kurt. "She's at work. Isn't she?"

Confused, Dana asked, "When was the last time you saw her?"

Turning away from the door, Marci shrugged. Her actions invited them inside. "I'm pulling night shift. She's gone when I get off, and I usually split before she gets home. Works out great. No fighting over the bathroom. Is something the matter?"

"She wasn't at work today. I was hoping you knew where she was."

"You're kidding." Marci put down the yogurt. "She never misses work. Should we worry?"

"I'm sure she's all right. There have been some problems at work. I need to talk to her."

Marci blinked rapidly and chewed first one side of her lip then the other. "Gosh, Dana, I've barely seen her lately. The only thing we say anymore is 'hi' and 'goodbye.'"

Kurt was looking at the telephone. Rubbing the back of his neck, he appeared a little too nonchalant. He nodded slightly and moved his eyes, indicating the door.

Catching his eagerness to leave, she said, "Thanks, Marci. If you should see her before I do, ask her to call me."

Once outside, she asked him why he'd wanted to leave. He said he'd show her. They went back to his car. He picked up his mobile phone and punched in a number. He listened for a moment and a slow smile appeared.

"Can I get where you're located?" As he listened, he reached around in the mess on the back seat and came up with a map. "I appreciate it. Thanks." He pressed the off button.

"What is this all about?"

He opened the map and studied it a moment. "Carl's at the Handi-Lodge Motel. Room twelve."

Amazed and delighted, she asked, "Now, how did you do that?"

"I saw a phone message saying to call Carl." He started the engine. "Let's roll. We'll probably find Jilly there, too."

Chapter Fifteen

Kurt knocked on the door to room twelve at the Handi-Lodge Motel. It was a run-down little tourist joint off Highway 75. The white paint on the walls was peeling, and the sidewalks were cracked. The humming of window-mounted air conditioners was almost as loud as the traffic zooming past on the highway. The pool looked as if it hadn't been used in years. Kurt doubted if the room rate was more than twenty bucks a night.

The draperies over the window moved. He knew Carl and Jilly were inside. Dana had recognized both their cars in the parking lot.

"Talk to them," he told Dana.

Dana rapped lightly on the door. "Jilly? Carl? Open up, please. We're all in trouble here, and we need one another. Jilly, please. I found out what Pauline did. I won't let her get away with it. I have Kurt Saxon with me. He's an excellent attorney."

Nothing.

"What now?" she asked. "We can't very well break down the door."

"Talk some more."

She drew a deep breath and knocked again. "Carl, I got your pictures. They didn't arrive until Thursday. I saw what Dragon-man did to your home. I know he hurt you. We're here to help, but you have to let us in. You have to tell us what it means."

Kurt rubbed her back in encouragement.

"I didn't shoot Eddie Gordon. I didn't know about him at all until I was arrested. But Dragon-man thinks I killed him, and now he's after me, too."

A sleepy-looking man walked out of the adjacent unit. He eyed them incuriously before heading for the office.

The door opened a crack. A worried blue eye peered out.

"Oh, Jilly, please let us in," Dana said.

"You told Pauline about the pictures. You tell her everything." Her voice quavered with accusation.

"No...no. I know I was wrong about Carl. I found out this afternoon what Pauline did to you, and I know why you were trying to take files. I understand."

"She fired Sue, too."

"You and I have always been good friends. You're the best secretary I've ever had. I would never do anything to hurt you. Please let us in."

Jilly looked up at Kurt. From behind her, a man said, "Go ahead, honey. Let them in."

When they entered, Kurt waited a moment for his eyes to adjust to the dimness. At the sight of Carl Perriman, he nearly whistled. Both eyes were blackened. His arms and neck were marked by brownish shadows of what had been extensive bruising. White tape held his glasses together at the nosepiece.

Dana looked ready to cry. "Oh, Carl, look what he did to you."

Kurt extended his right hand. "Hello, Carl. Kurt Saxon."

The younger man hesitated but finally shook hands.

Jilly's eyes filled with tears. "You should have seen him before. He looked like the Elephant Man. They knocked out two of his teeth."

"I'm okay." He lisped slightly. "I got away. They were going to kill me."

"Why didn't you go to the police?" Dana clenched her hands over her belly.

"I was scared. If I told the police about those men, I'd have to tell them..." His face turned bright red. "I've been doing some things that are kind of...illegal. Do you swear Pauline didn't send those men after me?" He looked between her and Kurt.

The room had a bed, a cheap desk and a single chair. Sensing Carl's intimidation, Kurt sat on the chair, and the young man seemed to relax slightly without Kurt towering over him.

"I can't swear it a hundred percent, but we don't think so. What kind of illegal things?"

Carl gazed sideways with a sheepish expression. "I followed her. I—I bugged her telephone."

"He didn't do it, I did it," Jilly said. She lifted her head defiantly. "I put the thingamabob in her phone. Carl didn't break in or anything. She's a thief, Dana. Carl never forged those checks, she wrote them herself. She also buys supplies, then returns them for refunds and keeps the cash."

Kurt fought down a laugh; amateurs, had to love them. "Carl, this isn't about Pauline, it's about the pictures you took. Eddie Gordon was a drug dealer. Dragon-man is probably one, too, or something worse. I think you took pictures of some kind of transaction."

Dana produced the snapshots. She showed Carl the men in the background.

Looking shocked, Carl sank onto the bed. Jilly sat beside him and held his hand. The young lovers exchanged a look of mingled fear, confusion and wariness. "I don't remember any men," Carl said.

"They remember you. Or at least, Dragon-man does. Where did you take these?"

"White Rock Lake."

"Neal lives near there," Dana said.

"Be more specific. That's a big lake." Kurt found his notebook and turned to a clean sheet.

"Not actually at the lake, it was north in the park. Um, White Rock Creek Park."

"Mr. Harlow's been seeing Pauline a long time," Jilly said, and blushed. "Even while he was dating you, he used to, you know, flirt with her and she'd flirt with him. When you weren't around, they'd go into her office and shut the door. I didn't want to say anything to you, Dana. I mean, it was none of my business, and besides, you know how Pauline is."

"Never mind. I don't care about her and Neal."

Kurt caught the strained note of embarrassment in Dana's voice. Maybe he'd go ahead and beat up Neal Harlow, anyway, just to make them both feel better.

"Go on, Carl. Tell me about the pictures. What day was it?"

"March 12, a Saturday."

Dana gasped. She immediately shut her mouth, but hot color rose in her cheeks.

"You're sure about the date?" Kurt asked.

"I'm sure. I'm keeping a notebook. It was late afternoon, kind of rainy and gray. The park was pretty much deserted. I only had one roll of film with me, so that's all the pictures I took."

"Did you see anyone else in the park?"

Carl stared at a photograph. "I wasn't paying attention to anybody except Pauline. It was a pretty crummy day. Cold, windy. I wasn't there very long. Maybe twenty minutes. Sneaking around in the bushes got me wet, and I couldn't get close enough to hear what they were saying. I got kind of scared, too. A couple times, all they had to do was turn around and they would have seen me. So I left."

"Then what?"

"I got the pictures developed and had two prints made. I didn't really want to send them to you, Dana. I wasn't sure how you felt about Neal. I kept waiting to hear from you, and when I didn't, I figured you were mad at me. Or that you had confronted Pauline and she'd made up some story you fell for."

"Oh, Carl, I do believe you. I didn't get the pictures until ten days after you mailed them. I didn't even open the envelope. I was arrested and I forgot about them. That is, until Dragon-man showed up."

"I didn't mean to tell them I sent you the pictures," he mumbled.

Kurt urged him to tell them about Dragon-man and Eddie Gordon.

"It was Tuesday. I was eating breakfast, reading the paper. These men came to the door. They forced their way inside. They hit me." He shuddered and paled. "The tall one held me while the other one..." He straightened on the chair and lifted his shirt, revealing a faded rainbow of bruises.

Dana covered her mouth with a hand. Kurt's stomach knotted.

"They kept talking about the pictures. I didn't know what they were talking about until they found the pictures I'd taken of Pauline. They knew my name. That's why I think it's Pauline who sent them. How would they know my name otherwise?"

Kurt glanced up from his notes. "Could be they saw you, followed you to your car and tracked you down through your license plate number. Go on."

"They tied me up with tape. They said they'd be back. I know they meant it. They were going to come back and kill me. I was never so scared in my life."

"I imagine," Kurt mused. "Can you identify these men? Give a description?"

Carl's eyes lit up with fierce light. "The tall one, he's the one who—" He glanced at Dana and looked away. "He's the one who was killed. I recognized his face in the newspaper."

"I didn't kill him, Carl. I wasn't even there."

"That's another story," Kurt interrupted. "What about the other man, Carl?"

"The one guy kept calling him Drag. He's not much taller than me, maybe five foot eight, but he's big. Real muscular. He's an older guy, maybe forty or forty-five, and his hair is going gray. His face is pitted with acne scars. He's got tattoos on his hands." He passed a finger over his knuckles. "I'll never forget his hands. One side said Love and the other said Hate."

"Did they give you any idea why they wanted the pictures?"

"It had to have been Pauline—"

"It wasn't. If it had been her, they'd have taken more than the pictures. Dana and I found the items you took out of Pauline's trash. The only thing those goofs wanted were the pictures. Did they ever mention Pauline's name? Or Neal's?"

"No."

"Why beat you up to get Dana's name? If Pauline knew what you were up to, wouldn't she have realized you'd send information to Dana?"

"Well, I suppose so."

"Think, did they say anything else?"

"Drag, he kept talking and talking, but I don't remember exactly what he was saying." He fingered his face. "He wanted the pictures."

"Dragon-man has to be the man in the background," Dana said.

The young man looked near tears. He eyed Dana mournfully. "All I ever wanted to do was prove to you I'm not a thief."

"I am so sorry for ever doubting you. I'll make it up to you. You, too, Jilly."

"Worry about that later," Kurt said. "Our immediate concern is Dragon-man. Carl, I'm taking you to the police station. Don't worry about the surveillance, nobody cares."

"Will they believe him?" Dana asked. "You can't see faces, there's no telling who those men are in the pictures."

Kurt's beeper went off. He checked the number. It was a friend of his who worked at the courthouse. The message said urgent. "I'm going out to my car to make a call. Be back in a minute."

ALONE WITH CARL AND JILLY, Dana didn't know what to say. The three of them remained still and silent, as uncomfortable as the shabby room warranted. Dana stared at a hideous landscape hanging on the wall. Its muddy colors seemed to say, sleep for the night, but don't linger here.

Finally, Dana said, "I'm sorry about all this. I realize now I treated you terribly, Carl. I don't know how to make up for it." She sat on the chair. "But why didn't you tell me?"

Carl and Jilly gazed at each other. It was Jilly who spoke. "Pauline is your best friend. You believe everything she tells you. She lies all the time. She's ruthless and mean. When she makes mistakes, she blames it on other people, and you always believe her. She takes money out of petty cash. She steals. You never notice."

"Pauline told me," Carl said, "if I pushed it, she'd prosecute me. Put me in jail. She would, too. She knows I caught her stealing, and she knows I can't prove it."

Dana pinched the bridge of her nose against the urge to cry.

"I don't like Pauline and she doesn't like me," Jilly said. "Everybody knows it. You know it. I was scared if I said anything about her, you'd think I was just being mean."

The sad part was, they were probably right. Self-loathing made Dana cringe.

Kurt pounded furiously on the door. Dana sprang to answer.

"We got problems," he said. "Callister and Tannenbaum have an arrest warrant, and this time they mean business. They found some kind of evidence."

She'd never seen him so furious. "How? What?" she whispered.

"I don't know, but it's serious." A string of curses flowed from him like a rushing river.

Dana's heart pounded. "We have Carl. And what about Patty? She'll tell them Dragon-man was there."

"Carl is extraneous. Even if they believe his story, it doesn't place Dragon-man at O'Dooley's. It doesn't do anything about the eyewitnesses or the videotape. As for Patty, she's probably the evidence they have. I bet she went to the cops."

"But Dragon-man, he was there. She said it's self-defense."

"She told them you were running and fired the shot. They now have a witness to the actual shooting."

She snatched a photograph off the bed. "We have pictures."

He studied the photograph. "Even if we get this to a lab and have it blown up, the graininess will kill any chance of identifying—"

Dana grabbed his arm. "If a photo lab does it, yes, but what about computer enhancement? Computers can do incredible things. I bet we can make those images big enough for identification."

Kurt looked more than interested. His gray eyes fairly danced with excitement. "How long will it take?"

"Do you know how to do it?" Jilly asked. "I don't want you going to jail. They can't do that to you." Her face skewed in a bewildered grimace.

Dana smiled grimly. "I don't know how to do it, but I know somebody who does. And she owes me."

"HELLO, PAULINE, glad you could make it," Dana said. In the Star Systems reception area, she sat on Jilly's chair and had her feet propped atop the secretary's desk.

The redhead looked between Dana and Kurt. For once, she wasn't batting her eyelashes in the presence of a good-looking man. For once, she looked scared. "What's this all about, Dana? You said it's an emergency."

"You might call it that." She surprised herself. Instead of pain or regret, all she felt was cold anger. "I've come to a decision. I'm going to sell out my half of Star Systems. It's all yours."

"What's this all about?"

"Isn't that what you wanted? For half the money I make, you can hire a sales staff. You'll be the boss, and if you want to milk this place dry, it won't be stealing. It'll all be yours."

Pauline's throat worked convulsively. "You're not making any sense. Have you gone crazy? You've been talking to Jilly. That little sneak! She's lying. She's the thief, not me."

"I know all about it. You framed Carl. You took the money, not him. You've been doctoring the books, falsifying invoices, changing the billing, stealing from petty cash and making Jilly cover for you." She dropped her feet to the floor. "I thought I knew you."

"You can't prove any of it—"

"Oh, yes, I can. I can call in an independent auditor to go over this place item by item, piece by piece. I can give the employees polygraph examinations and find out who's covering for you. I can file a lawsuit and make you produce bank statements, tax records, the works."

Pauline dropped onto a chair and covered her face with her hands.

"There's another thing I'm curious about. Why Neal Harlow? How long have you been using him to find a way to force me out?"

Pauline flung up her head. "Now you're being damned crazy! That thing with the morals clause was just to pacify clients. Good gawd, the business is going down the tubes here. We're losing Chusak, did you know that? Their lawyers are saying their data can be used as evidence if you go to trial. So they're pulling out. That's your fault, Dana, not mine. I'm trying to fix things."

"So what were you and Neal discussing on March 12?" She held up the photograph of Neal and Pauline kissing.

Staring wide-eyed, Pauline shook her head. Her face paled and her freckles looked painted on. "That doesn't mean squat. You and Neal broke up—"

"There you're wrong. Neal and I had a date that night. He said he was sure he loved me and suggested we move in together."

"He told me you weren't seeing each other."

"You are lying." She laughed wearily. Pauline seemed so transparent; how had she fooled Dana all those years? "The first thing I did on Sunday morning was call you up and cry on your shoulder. Remember? You agreed wholeheartedly that Neal Harlow was a complete jerk."

She held up photographs one by one, taking Pauline on a little stroll down memory lane. "Here's what I think happened. You knew Neal and I were growing close, and you were jealous. So you came on to him, maybe you slept with him. Except he and I kept dating, and he was falling in love with me. You listened to him complain about how I wouldn't have sex with him. You sympathized. You planted the bug in his ear. Commitment, you said, that's what Dana wants, knowing full well he wasn't ready to get married, and there's no way I'd move in with him. You knew something like that would break us up."

"You are so full of crap." Naked hatred blazed from Pauline's eyes.

"It doesn't matter if I'm right or wrong." She turned a photo around and clucked her tongue. "Actually, it does matter. I've been wrong about you all along. I never should have trusted you. You're a liar and a thief, and you're cruel. You use people. You're as cold and calculating as those machines you love so much."

"Let's do it, Dana," Kurt said. "We're running out of time."

"I need a favor, Pauline."

"After what you—"

"You're going to do it." Dana wondered if she shouldn't feel guilty about feeling so good. "Because if you don't, I will destroy you. I will tangle you up in lawsuits until the only men you ever talk to are attorneys and judges. You will lose Star Systems forever." She held up the photograph of Pauline and Neal kissing. "There are three men in the background. I need to see their faces."

"You can't—'

"If you do help, then we'll work out a deal so you can buy me out. A very generous deal. I'm willing to take a loss just so I never have to see your face again."

Pauline jumped off the chair and grabbed the photograph. She scowled at it. "How'd you get this, anyway? Did you hire a private eye to spy on me? And you call me a sneak?"

"It's a long story, and quite frankly, you don't deserve to hear it. Let's go."

In the computer room, Dana and Kurt gave Pauline room to work her magic. She scanned the first photograph into the computer.

"You're sure she can do this?" Kurt whispered in Dana's ear.

"If she can't, then it's impossible. Watch."

He found her hand and clasped it. He smiled approval. "You did good, babe. How do you feel?"

"I'll probably feel terrible later, but right now—" she glared at Pauline's back "—it feels marvelous."

Pauline isolated the men in the background with a computer-drawn box. A click of the mouse made the rest of the picture disappear. Increment by increment, she increased the image size, cleaning and enhancing it in stages. Faces grew distinct as the computer filled in features and interpreted what lay behind the shadows.

Twenty minutes later, Pauline scooted back her wheeled chair. "How's that?"

The enhanced image showed three men huddled together. The man in the middle was in profile; the man on the right was captured with three-quarters of his face visible; the third man, standing on the left, had his back to the camera.

Kurt touched an image of the man on the right. "That's definitely Dragon-man."

"That could be Gordon on the left. Do you have any idea who the man in the middle is? I sure don't. Print it, Pauline, then do the same with the other pictures."

"What's going on here?" Pauline asked as she began working on the second photograph. Her belligerence had disappeared as she warmed to her task. Her fingers were a blur on the keyboard. She manipulated the mouse as if it were an extension of her brain, making it seem as if all she had to do was think about a command and the computer executed it. "Isn't Gordon the guy you killed?"

Dana could have slapped her.

It was well after two in the morning when Pauline finally finished. Dana gathered all the printouts and photos in a folder. She didn't know what they had, but she and Kurt agreed that if Dragon-man was so eager, then the police most likely could figure it out.

"I won't be back, Pauline. Any further contact I have with you will be through an attorney."

Chapter Sixteen

"You're an amazing woman," Kurt said as he parked his car next to Dana's inside her garage. "How do you feel?"

Good question, Dana thought wearily. It was nearly three in the morning—she was practically numb. "Exhausted, mostly. Scared. Foolish for being so dumb about Pauline. Vindicated. Relieved. Kind of sad. A little bit of everything, I suppose." She slid her hand across the seat and found his. She touched him with her little finger, enough for comfort. "I'm so glad you're with me. I don't know what I would have done without you."

He chuckled. "You're worth it."

"But not worth getting back in the saddle again." As soon as the words left her mouth, she wanted to take them back. She wanted Kurt's friendship. Throwing his words in his face wasn't very friendly. She shook her head. "I'm sorry. I'm tired. I didn't mean that." She reached for the door handle.

"Sure you did. I'm the one who told you not to lie to your attorney." He heaved a deep breath. "I guess ravishing you tonight is out of the question."

Her throat tightened. She didn't want it to be the truth. "I care about you a lot." She made herself look at him. He was solemn, watchful. "But I want, need, different things than you do. I could go to bed with you right now. You are an exciting, desirable man, and I am so very grateful to you, and so...alone. But those are the wrong reasons."

He scratched his chin and fiddled with the steering wheel. "Love and all that jazz." He may have meant to sound light, but his words held a mournful note.

"I'll get married someday. I want children, I want someone to grow old with. I'll never be satisfied with less. And that's the whole truth."

The corners of his mouth curved. "One night. I'll change your mind."

It was tempting, but she knew what would happen. They'd become lovers, they'd date and have fun and engage in ridiculous conversations, and he'd annoy her, challenge her, argue with her, delight and surprise her. She'd fall in love. She'd desperately want him to fall in love with her. She'd grow demanding, start pressuring him for a commitment, and he'd resist until the pressure grew unbearable.

He'd break her heart.

"The only thing I'd be doing would be trying to change your mind, and I don't think that will happen."

The garage door light winked off, plunging them into darkness. The ticking of the cooling engine and chirping crickets sounded very loud. Dana dug through her purse to find the garage door remote unit.

"How about dinner tomorrow night, then? I'm going to take you to the Greek place."

She activated the remote, and the light came back on as the door rumbled down. "I'll probably be in jail."

"What, no faith in your white knight? No fair, I haven't given up on my fantasy girl yet. I won't let you go to jail."

She gathered the folder containing the pictures of Dragon-man. "I just wish we knew what these pictures meant. It still sounds like a wild story."

"You won't go to jail, babe. You have my word on that." He twisted on the seat and started rummaging around in the back seat.

"What are you looking for?"

"A clean shirt. Judges always like me better when my clothes are clean. Do you have an iron?"

Laughing, she left the car. She stretched her aching back and rolled her shoulders. She needed sleep and lots of it. Tomorrow she faced the biggest sales job of her life: convincing the police she wasn't a killer. She turned on the overhead lights for Kurt and entered the house.

She noticed the glass as soon as she turned on the kitchen light. Glittering shards littered the carpet at the base of the French doors leading to the backyard. She lifted her gaze slowly. The pane nearest the door handle had been broken.

Her heart leapt into her throat. She turned around to call Kurt. Dragon-man pounced from behind the kitchen counter.

In pure reflex, she swung wildly with the folder. She smacked the man squarely in the face. Papers and photographs burst free like oversize confetti. He shouted. She screamed and ran for the back door.

Crack! Glass exploded. Dana ducked and covered her head with her arms. Sobbing, she stumbled around the couch, hit the coffee table and went sprawling to the floor. She scrambled to her hands and knees, seeking frantically for any place to hide.

Snooky yowled like a banshee and shot from beneath the coffee table. Every hair standing on end, the cat launched himself over the couch.

Dragon-man yelled in surprise.

Crack!

Dust and plaster puffed from the ceiling.

She rolled under the coffee table. Curled in the tightest, smallest ball she could form, she gasped and shivered.

And waited. She was going to die. Dragon-man was going to kill her and Kurt, and they'd bleed all over her carpets.

Unfair! There were too many things she needed to do. She hadn't had time to tell her parents she understood about the adoption and she still loved them. She still hadn't met her sister. She'd never know for certain if Kurt could love her.

She heard a thud. She waited some more. Was he out of bullets? What had happened to Kurt?

"Dana?" Kurt asked in a fearful whisper. "Oh, God, Dana, baby, where are you?"

"Here," she squeaked, and wriggled from beneath the table. How she got under it in the first place, she couldn't imagine, since it was low and narrow, catching on her hips and legs. It bumped and clattered.

Kurt grasped her arm and helped her upright. In one hand, he held a baseball bat. With the other, he caught her in a tight embrace, burying his face against her hair. She clung to him. She could feel his heart pounding as if it would beat free of his chest.

"I'm all right, I'm okay," she said breathlessly. "He didn't hit me. I'm okay."

The air smelled bitter with gunpowder.

She peered slowly past his shoulder.

Dragon-man lay on his face, perfectly still.

Nausea rose in her throat. No dead men in her house—*please!* "Did you shoot him?" she whispered.

"Nah." He hefted the bat. "I ever tell you aside from being a great catcher, I'm also one hell of a slugger?" His eyes narrowed, as hateful as his smile. "I owed him one. Carl owes him one, too. Got any duct tape?"

Dana didn't have duct tape, but she did have a role of heavy-duty, nylon-threaded shipping tape. Kurt and Dana made quick work of taping Dragon-man hand and foot. By the time they were finished, he was groaning and his eyelids fluttered. Kurt turned his face toward the light and studied his eyes.

"He'll live," he announced, and dropped his hold. Dragon-man's head thunked on the floor.

Dana called the police. Surprised, and proud, of how calm she felt, she explained the situation. She hung up. "They're on their way. What are you doing?"

Kurt rifled through Dragon-man's pockets. Fully awake, the man glared daggers. "Looking for ID. He isn't much of a dragon anymore. More like a toad."

"I'm going to kill you, clown," Dragon-man sputtered. "You're dead meat."

Kurt produced two wallets. One was old, the brown leather rubbed yellow in spots; the other was thin and black. He opened the black wallet and his eyes widened. Whistling, low and wondering, he showed Dana a gold detective's shield. "If this goof is a cop, I'll quit my job and actually join the circus."

"I'm gonna chop you up and feed you to the hogs, clown boy. You and her. You're both dead meat. You better sleep with one eye open the rest of your damned lives."

Kurt kicked him lightly. "Shut up or I'll tape your face and you won't have to shave for weeks."

Dana touched the badge. "The way my luck is running, Kurt, he is a police officer."

"I doubt it." He opened the other wallet. "Look here. Say hello to Augustus Ponchet of Alexandria, Louisiana. So what are you doing with a gold shield, Gus? Did you and Eddie have a little scam going? Maybe ripping off drug dealers? You flash a badge, take the money and the dope, tell them to be good boys and turn them loose. Am I close? You can answer now."

Dragon-man told him, quite crudely, what the attorney could do with his theories.

A lone police officer arrived, but before he could step inside the house, two more patrol cars turned into the cul-de-sac. Dana doubted if she'd get any sleep tonight.

Kurt told her to sit and stay out of the way. She pulled a stool into the kitchen, sat on it and watched the proceedings with interest. The police officers seemed amused by Dragon-man's taped condition.

Two started a lively debate about transporting him the way he was, or cutting him free and using handcuffs.

Kurt showed them the door where Dragon-man had broken in and pointed out the bullet hole in the ceiling and in the French door. He gave them a terse, dry recounting of what had happened.

An officer accepted Dragon-man's gun and two wallets. He looked at the badge. His eyes widened; blood drained from his cheeks. He gasped, his mouth opening and closing, and he made alarming little coughing sounds as if he was choking. His face turned bright red. He sputtered, "Don't touch him!"

Alarmed, Dana straightened on the stool.

The three officers moved as a group further into the family room. They spoke in hushed, excited voices. Dana caught "Supervisor" and "Detectives" and several times the warning "Keep the hell away from him."

Did Dragon-man have some sort of horrible transmittable disease? An officer ordered her and Kurt into the dining room. Giving Dragon-man wide berth, he caught both of them by the elbow and physically herded them into the other room and closed the doors.

"What in the world is going on?" she whispered.

"Something hot," Kurt replied, standing to the side of the door and watching the activity between the kitchen and family room. "Hmm, they're looking at the pictures now. Might as well sit down. Looks like we're in for a wait."

Dana eventually dozed. The next thing she knew, Kurt was shaking her shoulder. She raised her head from the tabletop. Her neck creaked. Daylight streaming through the windows made her blink painfully.

Callister and Tannenbaum met her sleepy gaze. Seeing them snapped her wide awake. Her insides knotted. She wanted to run. After all she'd been through, now she faced arrest, booking, Callister calling her a liar and possibly being locked up in jail.

Callister smiled. His smile erased the bird-of-prey look from his face. He was almost pleasant-looking. Stunned and wary, Dana rose, resisting the urge to stretch her aching muscles.

She peeked at her watch. It was after nine o'clock. No wonder she was so achy.

"Coffee's ready," Kurt said.

She tugged at her rumpled clothing. "May I shower and change my clothes before..." She breathed deeply to steady herself. "Before you arrest me?"

Kurt chuckled.

Tannenbaum extended a hand. "We owe you an apology, Dana."

She shook hands automatically. His grasp was warm and friendly. "What's going on?"

"The gun we gave them," Kurt explained. "It's the weapon used to kill Eddie Gordon. Dragon-man shot his own partner."

She looked from face to face, astonished and half fearing she was still asleep and only dreaming this. "Dragon-man killed Gordon?"

"That's right. He must have popped off a shot during the struggle and hit Gordon. And Neal Harlow's gun turned up, too. Seems he discovered he'd only 'misplaced' it. Come on, let's get you some coffee. There's more.'' Kurt hooked his arm with hers and escorted her to the kitchen.

There she listened incredulously as the detectives told her about Dragon-man, Eddie Gordon and an undercover narcotics detective named Jerry Thurlow.

While investigating a drug connection, Detective Thurlow had been murdered on March 12 in White Rock Creek Park. His body was dumped in the bushes. With no leads and scant physical evidence, Callister and Tannenbaum had been working nearly around the clock trying to solve the murder. Now they had photographs showing Dragon-man and Gordon with Detective Thurlow in the park on the day in question, the nine-millimeter used to kill Gordon was the same weapon used to murder the policeman, and the shield Dragon-man had in his possession belonged to Detective Thurlow.

"I've spoken to Carl Perriman on the telephone,'' Tannenbaum said. "He's going to give us a full statement, and he's willing to testify at the trial. There will be no plea bargaining in this one. Dragon-man is a cop killer. We're going for the death penalty.''

The doorbell chimed. Kurt frowned in the direction of the front door. "Probably reporters.''

"I don't wish to speak to anyone until I've had a shower,'' Dana said. "Especially not the press.''

"I'll get rid of them.''

As soon as Kurt left the room, Callister propped an elbow on the counter and rested his chin on his fist. Through a closed expression, he regarded Dana. "There's one thing I just don't get. Why do you keep denying you were at O'Dooley's?''

Incredulous, Dana laughed. "You are beyond belief, Detective. After all I've been through, you still don't—"

"Perhaps I can explain." Star Jones walked into the room.

Tannenbaum choked and spewed coffee across the counter. Callister's chin slipped off his fist. He caught himself and jerked upright. Behind Star, Kurt and Austin smiled.

Dana whispered, "Star."

Except for her clothes, blue jeans, a T-shirt and a denim jacket, and her hair, which was cut very short and worn brushed back, it was like looking at a mirror image.

Star nodded at Austin. "I got in from my run last night and Mr. Tack here told me what's going down. I take it you fellas are the cops?" Her accent was thick as the heart of Texas.

"Who the hell are you?" Callister squeaked. He cleared his throat. "What are you? Twins?"

"I reckon that's right," Star said. "I was the woman at O'Dooley's. Only I didn't know that cretin got himself shot. I never fired." She produced a pistol strapped in a holster and a sheaf of paperwork. "Here's my gun and my permit. Haven't fired it in three, four months. Not since the last time on the range. Didn't shoot anybody. Never have."

"Not necessary," Callister said, sounding thoroughly confused. "Why did you flee the scene?"

Star slowly lowered her eyelids and lifted an eyebrow. Her expression said he'd asked the stupidest question she ever heard. "I had over six grand in cash stuck in my money belt and a car full of gold jewelry.

I'm supposed to wait around for those cretins to hit me again? I thought they were trying to rob me.'' She focused a mild, amused look on Dana. "You didn't show, so no sense sticking around. I got the hell out of Dodge.''

DANA BROUGHT ANOTHER pitcher of lemonade to the family room. Her father and Carl Perriman were trading fishing tales, for which she was grateful. Ever since she'd explained to her father about Pauline, he'd been talking nonstop about Dana taking over the operation of Benson Realty. Her mother sat on the couch between Jilly and Star, telling them about her latest charity work. Dana refilled glasses.

It was a lovely gathering and a lovely day. She had all the windows open to draw in a cool breeze. Birds were singing. The smoky scent of a charcoal grill still lingered from their barbecue.

The only thing missing was Kurt.

Dana missed him terribly. He'd cleared his belongings from her home and moved back to his office, she supposed. Her house was clean and tidy again—it felt sterile and empty and much too big. She even missed Snooky the cat.

She'd seen Kurt only once since Star walked into her life. That was when they all went down to the police station to give their official statements about O'Dooley's and Dragon-man. He'd been all business then, as brusque and commanding as when she'd first met him. Afterward, he'd promised to call.

He hadn't called.

Her own fault, she supposed. She'd made herself perfectly clear. No commitment, no fooling around.

No compromise.

Sighing, she returned to the kitchen.

Star joined her. "I'll help you clean up."

Dana smiled at her sister. Star had taken a vacation from her job, and they'd been trying to catch up on two lifetimes of separation. Unlike Dana, who remembered nothing of her life before the Bensons adopted her, Star had known all along she had a twin sister. For years she'd been searching for Dana. By chance, she'd seen a photograph of Dana in the society pages from when Dana had attended a charity Christmas ball with her parents.

According to Star, Dana's real name was Mary Jones, and her birthday was on Christmas Day. "Which stinks," Star had informed her, but found it amusing that Dana now had to accept she was thirty instead of twenty-nine. Star also remembered bits and pieces of their abandonment at the Dallas orphanage almost twenty-five years ago. She remembered a woman and a big car and a long drive in the night. Her memories were sketchy, though, and incomplete.

Dana remembered nothing. She felt Star's disappointment, but while she was curious in a detached sort of way, it was the Bensons who were her family. Her history was linked to them, not to people from a shadowy past.

It contented her having a sister in her life.

"You seem a little quiet," Star said. "Something wrong?"

"I'm fine." She scraped leftover potato salad into a plastic bowl.

"Hoping Kurt will show, I bet. Are you in love with him?"

Dana laughed. "Of course not. I barely know him."
So why did his failure to attend her barbecue hurt so
much? Why did she lie awake at night, wishing he were
still in her house? Why did everything remind her of
him?

"He's in love with you."

Dana laughed again. "Now you're being absurd.
He's my attorney, he helped me out. It was his job.
Besides, we aren't in the least bit compatible."

"Have you thought it over yet, princess?" Matthew Benson called. "Can we break out the bubbly
and celebrate Benson and Daughter Realty yet?"

Dana exchanged an exasperated look with Star. "I
still have to get the mess straightened out with Star
Systems. It'll take a while."

Matthew approached the kitchen. "You can work
on getting your broker's license in the meantime." He
jerked a thumb over his shoulder. "You can bring in
your own staff if you want. Bookkeeper, secretary,
whoever you want. Got free rein, princess. All you
have to do is say yes."

"Leave her be, Matt," Greta said.

"This is business, and business waits for no man. Or
girl. I've been waiting eight years to drag her on
board. That's long enough."

"Woman, Daddy. A grown-up woman. But if you
insist, I'll give you a definite answer no later than close
of business tomorrow. How about that?"

"Just as long as it's yes."

Everybody laughed. Jilly and Carl both sided solidly with Matthew. He wandered back to them, and
the three began discussing office renovations.

Dana thought she heard somebody call her name. She cocked her head. "Did you hear that?"

Bent over the dishwasher, Star asked, "Hear what?"

She heard it again. So did everyone else. All heads swiveled toward the front of the house. Dana wiped her hands on a towel and hurried to the front door. She couldn't imagine who in the world was out front shouting her name.

She flung the door open.

Kurt Saxon sat atop a cream-colored quarter horse gelding. The animal nibbled on a tea rose bush. Kurt, wearing a light gray suit and a dark red tie, sat stiffly on the saddle, holding the reins firmly in one hand. He cradled a bouquet of red roses.

Hand over her mouth, astonished, she approached him. "What in the world is this?"

"Dana, meet Barney. He's the closest I could find to a fiery white charger." He handed her the roses, then immediately grabbed the saddle horn. He looked as uncomfortable as a dog on a bicycle.

She pressed her nose against a velvety bloom. The sweet scent was heavenly. Barney swung his big head around and sniffed the roses, too. She stroked his soft nose. As Kurt's meaning sank in, a lump filled her throat. She lifted her gaze, meeting his sparkling gray eyes.

He certainly did know how to make a grand gesture.

"I thought you said you were never getting on a horse again. What was that you claimed? Getting back on after getting bucked off is a load of crap?"

"It's not as bad as I remember. But no sense pushing it. Hold his head, will you?"

She took the reins and Kurt dismounted. He brushed light-colored hairs off his slacks and smoothed back his hair. He grinned at her.

Star walked over to them. "It's true, I reckon. The straight chicks always attract the weirdos." Chuckling, she took the roses and reins from Dana. She led the horse closer to the house for Jilly and Carl to ooh and aah over.

Matthew and Greta stood side by side on the front porch. Greta fairly beamed her approval. Her father was trying hard, but failing, to hide his amusement.

Kurt took Dana's hand. "Walk with me for a minute."

"What's this all about?" she asked. She couldn't quite trust what her heart was saying. She needed to hear it from him.

"You're still my fantasy girl, babe. I've missed you." He squeezed her hand. "A lot."

"I've missed you. I kept hoping you'd call, but I didn't think you would."

He stopped on the sidewalk in front of her house and faced her. "I knew the first moment we met I could fall hard for you. But I never figured I'd fall in love."

She touched his face in wonder, making herself believe he was real. "You love me?"

"And you love me, too. Remember, no lying to your attorney."

She nodded happily. "I love you, Kurt."

"That's all I needed to hear."

He actually looked relieved, and Dana knew she'd spoken the pure, unadulterated truth. She loved this man with all her heart.

He kissed her, deeply, soulfully, thoroughly. A kiss that made her forget the hot sun on her back. A kiss of pure love. A kiss promising her the moon and the stars and his love forever.

After an eternity, he pulled away. He held both her hands and swung them gently between them.

Dana noticed their audience. Her parents, her sister, Jilly and Carl, her neighbors, and the horse. All of them smiled at her, except the horse.

"Let's go inside. I need a drink. My buddy will be by in a while to pick up his horse." He looped an arm around her shoulders and started across the lawn. "What time are your guests leaving? They need to be out of here by six. I've already made reservations, but don't ask, it's a surprise. Don't worry, you'll love it. Wear something spiffy."

She huffed in exasperation. "You're pretty darned demanding."

"So what's your point? We've already established I'm rude, crude and a bully, but you love me, anyway. So let's make it easy. Rule number one, fantasy girls don't argue with white knights. Especially when they're crazy enough to get on a horse."

"Says who? This is not a fairy tale, Kurt Saxon. This little princess isn't meek and mild, either. I'll have you know—"

He laughed and cut off her words with a kiss.

HARLEQUIN®

I N T R I G U E®

L.A. Law, look out! Here comes...

Harlequin Intrigue is thrilled to present M.J. Rodgers's exciting new miniseries, Justice Inc., featuring Seattle's legal sleuths. Follow this team of attorneys dedicated to defending the true spirit of the law—regardless of the dangers and desires in their way. Watch them take on extraordinary cases destined to become tomorrow's headlines...and to lead them to the love of a lifetime.

Don't miss the spectacular debut, coming this August:

BEAUTY VS. THE BEAST
Harlequin Intrigue #335

Available wherever Harlequin books are sold

JI-1

FLYAWAY VACATION SWEEPSTAKES!

This month's destination:

Glamorous LAS VEGAS!

Are you the lucky person who will win a free trip to Las Vegas? Think how much fun it would be to visit world-famous casinos... to see star-studded shows...to enjoy round-the-clock action in the city that never sleeps!

The facing page contains two Official Entry Coupons, as does each of the other books you received this shipment. Complete and return all the entry coupons—**the more times you enter, the better your chances of winning!**

Then keep your fingers crossed, because you'll find out by August 15, 1995 if you're the winner! If you are, here's what you'll get:

- Round-trip airfare for two to exciting Las Vegas!
- 4 days/3 nights at a fabulous first-class hotel!
- $500.00 pocket money for meals and entertainment!

Remember: The more times you enter, the better your chances of winning!*

*NO PURCHASE OR OBLIGATION TO CONTINUE BEING A SUBSCRIBER NECESSARY TO ENTER. SEE REVERSE SIDE OF ANY ENTRY COUPON FOR ALTERNATIVE MEANS OF ENTRY.

VLV KAL

FLYAWAY VACATION
SWEEPSTAKES
OFFICIAL ENTRY COUPON

This entry must be received by: JULY 30, 1995
This month's winner will be notified by: AUGUST 15, 1995
Trip must be taken between: SEPTEMBER 30, 1995-SEPTEMBER 30, 1996

YES, I want to win a vacation for two in Las Vegas. I understand the prize includes round-trip airfare, first-class hotel and $500.00 spending money. Please let me know if I'm the winner!

Name_____

Address _____ Apt. _____

City   State/Prov.   Zip/Postal Code

Account #_____

Return entry with invoice in reply envelope.

© 1995 HARLEQUIN ENTERPRISES LTD.   CLV KAL

FLYAWAY VACATION
SWEEPSTAKES
OFFICIAL ENTRY COUPON

This entry must be received by: JULY 30, 1995
This month's winner will be notified by: AUGUST 15, 1995
Trip must be taken between: SEPTEMBER 30, 1995-SEPTEMBER 30, 1996

YES, I want to win a vacation for two in Las Vegas. I understand the prize includes round-trip airfare, first-class hotel and $500.00 spending money. Please let me know if I'm the winner!

Name_____

Address _____ Apt. _____

City   State/Prov.   Zip/Postal Code

Account #_____

Return entry with invoice in reply envelope.

© 1995 HARLEQUIN ENTERPRISES LTD.   CLV KAL

OFFICIAL RULES

FLYAWAY VACATION SWEEPSTAKES 3449

NO PURCHASE OR OBLIGATION NECESSARY

Three Harlequin Reader Service 1995 shipments will contain respectively, coupons for entry into three different prize drawings, one for a trip for two to San Francisco, another for a trip for two to Las Vegas and the third for a trip for two to Orlando, Florida. To enter any drawing using an Entry Coupon, simply complete and mail according to directions.

There is no obligation to continue using the Reader Service to enter and be eligible for any prize drawing. You may also enter any drawing by hand printing the words "Flyaway Vacation," your name and address on a 3"x5" card and the destination of the prize you wish that entry to be considered for (i.e., San Francisco trip, Las Vegas trip or Orlando trip). Send your 3"x5" entries via first-class mail (limit: one entry per envelope) to: Flyaway Vacation Sweepstakes 3449, c/o Prize Destination you wish that entry to be considered for, P.O. Box 1315, Buffalo, NY 14269-1315, USA or P.O. Box 610, Fort Erie, Ontario L2A 5X3, Canada.

To be eligible for the San Francisco trip, entries must be received by 5/30/95; for the Las Vegas trip, 7/30/95; and for the Orlando trip, 9/30/95.

Winners will be determined in random drawings conducted under the supervision of D.L. Blair, Inc., an independent judging organization whose decisions are final, from among all eligible entries received for that drawing. San Francisco trip prize includes round-trip airfare for two, 4-day/3-night weekend accommodations at a first-class hotel, and $500 in cash (trip must be taken between 7/30/95—7/30/96, approximate prize value—$3,500); Las Vegas trip includes round-trip airfare for two, 4-day/3-night weekend accommodations at a first-class hotel, and $500 in cash (trip must be taken between 9/30/95—9/30/96, approximate prize value—$3,500); Orlando trip includes round-trip airfare for two, 4-day/3-night weekend accommodations at a first-class hotel, and $500 in cash (trip must be taken between 11/30/95—11/30/96, approximate prize value—$3,500). All travelers must sign and return a Release of Liability prior to travel. Hotel accommodations and flights are subject to accommodation and schedule availability. Sweepstakes open to residents of the U.S. (except Puerto Rico) and Canada, 18 years of age or older. Employees and immediate family members of Harlequin Enterprises, Ltd., D.L. Blair, Inc., their affiliates, subsidiaries and all other agencies, entities and persons connected with the use, marketing or conduct of this sweepstakes are not eligible. Odds of winning a prize are dependent upon the number of eligible entries received for that drawing. Prize drawing and winner notification for each drawing will occur no later than 15 days after deadline for entry eligibility for that drawing. Limit: one prize to an individual, family or organization. All applicable laws and regulations apply. Sweepstakes offer void wherever prohibited by law. Any litigation within the province of Quebec respecting the conduct and awarding of the prizes in this sweepstakes must be submitted to the Regies des loteries et Courses du Quebec. In order to win a prize, residents of Canada will be required to correctly answer a time-limited arithmetical skill-testing question. Value of prizes are in U.S. currency.

Winners will be obligated to sign and return an Affidavit of Eligibility within 30 days of notification. In the event of noncompliance within this time period, prize may not be awarded. If any prize or prize notification is returned as undeliverable, that prize will not be awarded. By acceptance of a prize, winner consents to use of his/her name, photograph or other likeness for purposes of advertising, trade and promotion on behalf of Harlequin Enterprises, Ltd., without further compensation, unless prohibited by law.

For the names of prizewinners (available after 12/31/95), send a self-addressed, stamped envelope to: Flyaway Vacation Sweepstakes 3449 Winners, P.O. Box 4200, Blair, NE 68009.

RVC KAL